THE UNTURNED STONE

SONIA ORIN LYRIS

KNOTTED ROAD PRESS

WANT MORE?

I announce new projects on my Facebook feed:

facebook.com/authorlyris

If you prefer very infrequent emails, sign up for my newsletter:

https://lyris.org/subscribe/

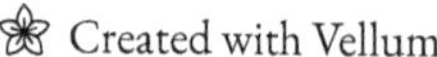 Created with Vellum

CHAPTER

ONE

Sanne woke suspecting the day would bring trouble. She lay in bed, staring at the ceiling, recalling her dream of cracking eggs into a bowl only to find them all lacking yolks. Empty.

Talk about symbolism.

Dreams were unreliable portents, often like drunk, dancing clowns: more interested in getting a rise out of the audience than saying anything of substance.

She kicked off the covers, rolled out of bed, and stretched, gazing out the window at the neighbor's house. All she could see was brick wall.

If she believed in omens, there was one.

But that was fuzzy, magical thinking, encouraging the clever mind to impose meaning where it was not. One must study the world as it was, if one intended to understand it.

The world as it was. Not as one wished it to be.

She pulled on sweatpants and sweatshirt, walked the few steps to the kitchen sink. Dreams might be clumsy sign-

1

posts, but if you paid attention, they sometimes pointed in useful directions.

Besides, she was in the mood for an omelet.

The first egg spilt its treasure into the white ceramic bowl without any fuss at all, the yolk's color a deep gold, spreading into the white, and really, saying nothing at all.

The second was another matter. The firm crack against the edge of the bowl sent bits of shell into the batter. Sanne muttered in frustration, fishing them out with a fork.

But did this mean anything more than that life was full of shards and mess?

She held the third egg in her left hand, the side of receiving, of contemplation, fingers curving gently over the pale shell. She whispered words that her mother had taught her when she was young, words of unmasking followed by a humble willingness to know more.

Next she transferred the egg to her right hand—action and decisiveness—and cracked it against the bowl, deftly spreading the halves with one hand to release its contents alongside the other two.

There it was: a blood spot. The shape was oblong, color vivid red. The yolk had broken on contact and the whole of the slimy yellow-orange swirl had a clear pattern: a tree, marked with red.

Nothing could be clearer. Sanne's trees—not her trees, of course, but she thought of them that way—were under threat. She must visit them as soon as she could.

She crushed the shell in her hands. A wet, sharp business. She opened her fingers and looked.

Three lines. A cross. Two dots.

No, this had nothing to do with the ancient grove. Someone had died.

There were doors of energy, locked and sealed, between her and her uncle, and so she did not expect to feel him as he crossed over into death.

Still, now, she knew.

The phone rang.

"Sanne," Marla said on the phone, then repeated herself, her voice choking.

Even if Sanne hadn't known, her sister's tone said everything.

"Jerry," Sanne said, reluctantly naming the uncle who had raised them.

Her sister inhaled, exhaled heavily. "He's gone. I can't believe it."

"I'm sorry," Sanne said. And she was. For Marla, anyway.

In memory, flames flickered, sparking an old anger.

Sanne and her uncle had fought from the first, after that horrific New Year's Eve when Sanne and Marla, eleven and ten, became orphans. Part of why Marla had become a lawyer, Sanne suspected: to serve up the justice that had somehow escaped the drunk driver.

Sanne had taken another path, learning everything she could about her mother's crafts: witch, wild, and other.

Jerry had taken the girls in, fed and sheltered them. He insisted they study hard. He pushed them to lucrative professions. When Marla went to law school, Jerry was proud.

Sanne dropped out after one term of college, abandoning a degree in computer science, declaring that she would teach herself.

"You little idiot," Jerry had snarled at her during their worst fight. "How are you going to pay rent? Just like your mother."

And proud to be.

She hadn't always been proud of that. It had taken Sanne years to find pride within. After their parents had died, Sanne became withdrawn. Jerry put her through years of therapy, trying to figure out what was wrong with her.

Nothing at all, Sanne finally realized.

Now, Sanne gripped the phone as memories cascaded, listening to Marla's quiet sob on the other end.

Sanne lived in a one-room house in the small town of Marigold, USA, tutoring kids and running occasional wildcrafting classes for eager wealthy suburbanites who were afraid they'd die if they ate the wrong mushroom. It wasn't much, but it covered the basics, and gave her time to do her real work.

As Marla talked, Sanne thought of Jerry. Her mind flashed to fire and outrage.

She had been twelve. A summer night, in the backyard, dim stars fighting through shreds of moonlit clouds. The three of them stood around the firepit. A place of good memories, of BBQs, marshmallows, and stargazing. Until that night.

Out of nowhere, Jerry railed at Sanne about her foolishness, make-believe, and lack of diligence. His disappointment.

In a rage, he took her craft books to the firepit and tossed them in. Worse, her personal notebooks detailing her studies, her memories of her mother. He shoved her away as she fought to get them out his hands, to pull them out of the fire.

Sanne was screaming, Marla was crying, and Jerry was burning her books.

Tears of fury streamed down her face as she watched the flames consume her treasure, watched her uncle burning even brighter in a way he himself didn't credit.

Over the years, Sanne had learned to push him away, keep herself apart. It was hard to do, living in the same house.

At last, she'd come to understand that Jerry, despite his protestations that magic didn't exist, could make a field around himself where magic, if not downright impossible, was very, very difficult.

Sanne left the morning of her sixteenth birthday, daring him, as she left him standing at the door, to have her brought back.

He didn't.

She left the town, then the state, then moved across country to get away from him.

The irony of her uncle wielding powerful magic while denying it existed was not lost on her. He could have been a witch. But it was hard to study a subject you thought was delusion.

They had not spoken in years. Now he was dead. After the flash of anger, all Sanne felt was relief.

However, her sister Marla, whom she loved, was hurting. Sanne went to the drying trellis. With her free hand, she reached overhead and took down a young bouquet of lavender stems and flowers bound with thyme.

"I'm sorry, Marla." Sanne traced runes in the air as she spoke, twirling the lavender-thyme bundle to make a healing spell. She pitched her tone to gentle care. "I love you, sister."

Marla laughed a little through tears, which told Sanne that even if Marla didn't know what it was, the spell had reached her.

"Enough to come home and help me sort out the storage units?"

Units, *plural*?

"Throw it all away. Better yet, burn it."

"Christ, Susanne, are you still upset about—"

"Hell yeah, I am."

Marla knew about Sanne's struggle with Jerry, but only the form, not the deeper substance. As far as Marla was concerned, Sanne and Jerry had fought about some sort of religion, and Marla was an atheist.

"I'll take care of it, Sanne," Marla said. "But if I find something of Mom's..."

"You won't," Sanne replied harshly, then regretted it. "You won't," she said again, more gently. "But if you do, keep it."

Sanne heard Marla's deep breath. "Gotta go, sis," Marla said. "I love you back."

TWO

Two thirteen-year-olds settled around Sanne's kitchen table, popping up the lids on their pricey laptops.

"You guys work on what I sent you?"

Their carefully blank expressions told her that they had not.

"Sure," said Rufus.

Sanne gave the flame-haired boy a sour yet amused expression. He lifted his chin in obvious mock defiance.

"Do it now," Sanne said lightly, and listened for a moment while they pattered on their keyboards.

She didn't even need to look to know if they were on social media or chatting. She could tell by how their fingers danced. No witchery there, just plain old paying attention.

They worked for a bit on the code she'd sent them as homework—a program to spit out primes, full of bugs that she wanted them to find. When they got stuck or frustrated, she gave clues and pointers, making them laugh while working in lessons on edge conditions and debugging practices.

They settled in. While they were working, Sanne slowly walked the room. She paused at the coat rack, overloaded with beat-up jackets and sweatshirts, and touched the scarf she'd just finished.

Red, orange, and green squares filled the length of it. She let her fingers follow a single strand of alpaca yarn woven through, wondering if llama would have been better for protection and sensitivity.

She felt the looks and turned back to the table. Rufus and Angie were watching.

"That's really cool," Angie said. "A Dr. Who scarf?"

"A what?" Sanne replied.

"No, a Who," Rufus said, laughing.

"Just a scarf," Sanne replied in a light tone that said there was nothing more to see here.

She almost breathed a few words of a look-away spell, but best not to do that when they were staring right at it. One never knew what someone might see.

"You made it?" Angie asked. "Teach us how!"

"You said you would," Rufus added accusingly.

Half-true. In a previous session, as the two kids were working an assignment, Sanne had started knitting. They watched her for a time, so Sanne threatened to teach them how, if they did not get back to work.

They weren't supposed to want to.

Rufus, never shy, bounded up from his chair and stood by the scarf, his hand kneading one of the ends as if he were a cat.

Get back to your work came to her to say, but got stuck in her throat at his intent gaze at the weave of the scarf.

Angie joined him, bent to pick up the other end. "Pretty," she said.

"You're here to learn to code," Sanne said.

"Rather knit," Rufus said stubbornly.

Sanne was entirely bemused. She didn't expect kids to have this fascination with knitting.

"Hundreds of vids on the internet," Sanne said. "Go watch them."

"But we want you to teach us," Angie said.

Such eagerness. Could they feel the spell in the scarf, perhaps not realizing that they did? She should have hidden the scarf before they came over.

"Can I try it on?" asked Rufus.

"No," Sanne snapped, her hand wrapping the scarf where it hung from the hook, making physical the boundary of her words.

It was not a word or tone she used often. Startled, they stepped back.

The scarf embodied knowledge. More precisely, it held a particular perspective on the world, and how it might work. It moved the wearer toward a deeper clarity. Sanne had worked the spell into the yarn for nearly a year, unstitching and restitching until the thing held together the way she wanted it to.

It was hardly something to wrap around the neck of an innocent.

Yet, their looks were expectant. Sanne tried to imagine explaining to their parents, who worked in technology, why she was teaching them to knit, in a class that was supposed to be about programming.

Something about multi-threaded concurrency, maybe. Sanne snorted softly, amused.

"Are those knitted, too?" Angie asked, excited.

Sanne followed the girl's gaze to the drying rack over the sink, from which hung all manner of plants, some loose, some bound, some braided, all to dry and be ready for use. Sanne harvested stems, leaves, flowers, and vines from the neighborhood or the wilds of Johan's land. Only with permission. The owner's attitude could grow into the plant.

No way around it: the kids felt the magic. They noticed the scarf, and at some level inside, unconsciously noticed that they had noticed.

Entirely unexpected. Was it this particular generation, more open to what they could not see? Or maybe she had just gotten lucky with these two.

"Can't support yourself knitting," Sanne said brusquely, gesturing at their laptops and the table to make the message stronger, a sick feeling in her gut as she heard with some revulsion her uncle's words coming out of her own mouth.

Rufus gave a frustrated exhale. Angie stared longingly at the scarf.

"Tell you what," Sanne said, relenting as she herded them back to the table, "finish this assignment. If we've got time before your parents come, I'll get out the needles and show you a basic stitch."

The kids sat quickly and got to work.

～

Angie and Rufus caught on to the basic stitch fast, their eagerness making Sanne smile.

There was no witchery in this teaching, no spell in their work beyond the human craving to create with one's hands.

To make a thing, to put your hands on the world with intention, was the beginning of magic. To make it formal and repeatable, you needed to know how your intention connected to everything else. Then it was a matter of study, experiment, of observation, testing, results, and repeatability.

These were the things Sanne had learned early on from her mother, before the night her parents had died. The notes she had taken on those lessons were the foundation of everything Sanne practiced, and those notebooks were the ones her uncle had burned.

Flames and witches, witches and flames.

She looked at the analog clock on the wall, which she had taught the kids to read, and told them to wrap up.

They grumbled. She reminded them about the programming homework, and urged them to see it like knitting—a thing to be made, less with the hands perhaps, but just as much a creation.

Did it sink in? She wasn't sure. They packed up their laptops. Sanne walked them to the curb to wait for their parents.

Angie's dad and Rufus's mother drove up at the same time, parked, and stepped out, small-town like, to say hello to each other.

Any hope Sanne might have had about keeping the knitting between the three of them vanished as Rufus opened his mouth.

"Can we buy needles on the way home?" Rufus asked his mother eagerly. At the woman's stunned look, Sanne winced.

"Sanne's teaching us to knit," Angie added enthusiastically.

The parents, as one, put their gazes on Sanne. She swallowed uncomfortably, almost reading their thoughts.

Not at these rates, she's not.

Sanne forced herself to return the look, smiling. There was, in their faces, at least slightly more confusion than hostility.

"Multi-threaded concurrency," Sanne said with brittle confidence, trying to recall which of these parents worked where, and on what, and failing.

Mercifully, Rufus and Angie moved quickly to another subject.

"Could we do a wildcrafting class with Sanne?" Angie asked.

"Out in the woods," Rufus added. "I'd learn lots!"

The air was suddenly full of talk of lunch, of soccer, and the school play. Sanne watched the adults' herd their young into cars, the knitting question set aside. At least for the moment.

Sanne waved as they all piled into vehicles. "See you next week!"

And they were gone. The street was quiet, delicate touches of bright green here and there, and the occasional eager bud in red, blue, and lavender, like the touch of an artist nearly out of paint.

Sanne ached for the forest, for the grove of ancient trees she considered her friends.

Did she have time? She glanced at her phone.
She had time.

THREE

SANNE PULLED INTO THE GRAVEL DRIVEWAY AND turned off the engine, at which point her beat-up Nissan made its usual mysterious clunking sound.

She touched the tip of the key with her finger and spoke a staving-off-illness spell that sometimes induced machines to good behavior, then gave three touches to the dashboard and a final one to the ignition.

"Just one more year, old girl, eh?"

She was saving up for a used pick-up truck, something to make it easier to bring native plants up here to Johan's land, to add variety to the edges of his forest, maybe even a few rare herbs.

Johan MacKenzie stood on his lawn, ever-present coffee mug in hand. He was talking to a couple dressed in clothes that marked them as city. The woman of the pair was gesturing in one direction, and then another, as she spoke.

Sanne, not wanting to interrupt, cast a quiet spell about herself as she circled wide, following the driveway into the meadow to the woods.

Maple, Douglas fir, alder, cedar. Here, in shade, the afternoon carried the sharpness of the cool night before, and the memory of winter now fading. She inhaled the elixir of early spring, the readying of fierceness of growth, the land gathering itself in the ages-old alchemy of sunlight, water, and soil, to create leaf, stem, branch. It was the pump of the world. It fed everything, including the spirit.

Sanne smiled at the richness of the air. As she came in sight of the great center tree and its siblings to either side, she took off her shoes, tucked socks in pockets, and hung the pair over her shoulder. She walked through the loam of years of fallen needles, circling huckleberry, patches of nettle sprouts, salal, and the crawling fingers of ground blackberry.

She circled wide around the three great trunks rising like pillars of giants. Touching the ground in four directions, she muttered a blessing for the land, the trees, and all who came here. Next she named the known tribes who had once lived on this land and had been forced to leave.

In each direction of the compass, she touched the ground, accepting the powers of north, west, east, and south.

She stepped close to the center tree, picking her way over the base of gnarled roots, and looked up through branches of evergreen. New growth was bright bolts of emerald.

Wordlessly, she gave a greeting to the three powerful, ancient creatures, then made herself quiet to hear their reply.

While her own litany was a bit grand, touching on joy

and sorrow, honor, respect, and humility, the trees' reply was simple.

We know you, child.

She felt a chill of delight, a wash of insight, a sense of returning home from the world that humans created with their hands and minds. She felt herself hum with aliveness. Dirt under her feet, a breeze on her face, and astonishment at being spoken to by a tree centuries old.

She had been coming here to Johan's forest for some seven years now, talking to this great old one and its siblings. This moment, hearing its voice, never became common. She was awestruck.

"May I approach?" she asked softly.

The answer came slowly, across minutes, like a bud unfolding through spring.

Yes. Touch.

Sanne's eyes filled with tears of joy as she came to the base of the wide tree, so wide she could not see one side from the other, the moss-covered bark wrinkled in lines of ages, having drawn from ground and sky, from fungus and insect and bird and mammal, to become this moment, to become itself.

As her fingertips brushed moss and fern over grooved bark, felt insects move beneath—a small world of activity— her chest shuddered in slight sobbing gasps, all the pain held in and buried, memories of her uncle but also of being misunderstood for who she was. All swirling up and out. And free.

Sanne put her hands and then her arms and then her chest to the tree, feeling the lives of all the creatures and plants that made their home here, where her cheeks and tears touched wood.

Touch, tears, breath, and then, finally, a kiss. The bark tasted of time and space, of life and death. It drew her in and gave her back to herself.

~

SANNE CAME OUT OF THE FOREST FEELING restored. While working with the kids was easy enough, adults were a bit challenging. She must always keep in mind what they could and couldn't understand, making sure to tidy her language of anything to do with the craft.

She was struck by the beauty of the moment. She resolved to visit more often. She'd get up at dawn, feel the land, hear the birds, speak with the trees.

The couple Johan had been speaking with were just now getting into a shockingly pink car, which Sanne imagined purred nicely until one turned it off, then was obediently silent.

The car backed up in the gravel driveway, wheels turning to aim at the paved road. The woman at the wheel swept her gaze across the house and lawn, garden and fence, and stopped briefly on Sanne.

Sanne felt a chill, and something sickly familiar: a dampening, or flattening, as if the fullness and heart she had taken from the forest were only dreams, dispersed in a gust of wind.

Momentarily locking gazes with the woman, Sanne felt her defenses: a hard, protective bubble. On top of that, a curtain of illusion—nothing to see here, just a quiet little stone. She brushed the woman's attention to pass her by.

The woman's eyes narrowed slightly but her gaze went to the road before her. The car crunched gravel, accelerated, and was gone.

Sanne exhaled slowly. She allowed the barriers to soften and dissipate. It was as if the color of life flowed into her, up from the ground.

Johan was ambling toward her. She met him on the lawn, cool grass underfoot.

He nodded a greeting. "How you doing, Susanne?"

"Making do," she answered, a common phrase in Marigold. "Yourself?"

"Oh, fine. Just fine."

But from his clouded expression, she could tell it wasn't so.

She smiled gently and waited.

He heaved a breath. "Yeah, not so good," he said softly. "Can't take care of them myself. The nurse isn't enough. Mom's cancer's back."

"Oh, Johan. I'm so sorry."

A short shrug. "The way things go sometimes. What are you going to do?"

"What are you going to do," she echoed softly.

He sniffed. "Anyway. Wanted you to know." His head nodded toward the road, and by implication the car that had just left. "We're just talking. Looking at options."

Just talking. Dread rose in Sanne.

"Real estate agents?" she guessed.

"Can't believe how much property around here is

worth now." He laughed a little, but there was no humor in it.

Johan's family had owned this hundred acres for four generations. They'd run a cow dairy with some milk goats. When big dairy made that financially impossible, they'd tried cannabis, which had its own set of problems, and he shut it down two years back. Now he grew spinach.

Thanks to good farming practices, and a little spell-casting from Sanne, the crops had performed magnificently. But it hadn't been enough.

Sanne had offered him money, though she didn't have much. He'd actually considered it, asked her how much she was offering, then laughed and told her to keep it.

"Johan," she said softly, "You always told me they'd have to take you out in a box."

Johan nodded vigorously. Then the motion slowed, turning into a headshake. "Mom needs surgery, and the damned insurance company won't. Well, it just won't." He met her gaze. "And dad wanders. Just wanders. I have to hide the car keys from him. My own father." He scowled through pain. "My kids can't help. Got problems of their own. Got to find another answer."

She'd move in, Sanne decided. Move her home here, tutor in the unused barn. Be cold in the winter, but she would find a way. More convenient for the wildcrafting classes, anyway.

"I can help," she said. "I could—"

He held up a hand. "You're generous, Susanne. Always been."

"The barn," Sanne insisted. "You're not using it. I could live there. Help out."

He sucked at his front teeth thoughtfully. "If that were enough, I might let you. But the house is already mortgaged to cover my kids' debts. What's left is going to mama's surgery. I need a lot more than you can scare up with your Wiccan ways."

Her shock must have shown. He smiled. "It's all right. Been Christian my whole life, and I've got my faith, and that's my business. You've got yours, and I respect that."

Sanne was both unnerved and touched. She wasn't Wiccan, but it was close enough.

"You're a good man," she said and it was heartfelt.

"I try, Susanne. I really do."

"But what makes you think that I'm…" she trailed off, not wanting to give any name to attach to what she was or wasn't.

He chuckled. "Your neighbor Donna Daley is in my church. She told me you saved her little Persian, Winston, one snowed-in Christmas eve, when the vet wouldn't answer."

"Just some healing herbs," Sanne said, shaking her head.

"Donna told me you said a spell. Asked me if I thought it was okay. Or if it was ungodly."

Ungodly. That was a word that could lead to ugly places.

Sanne remembered being called into the principal's office in high school to be asked about symbols spray painted on school walls. Not hers, she would never, but the fact that they called her in first was a lesson to be more careful about who knew what.

At least witches weren't burned any more. Just their books.

Sanne had thought Donna was in the other room, out of hearing, when she'd softly muttered that spell over the small cat.

Every spell had costs and benefits, subtleties to consider. A witch must be deliberate and thoughtful. Sometimes Sanne's focus on the occult made it easy to miss the social aspect.

She must be more careful.

"What did you tell her?" Sanne asked.

"Asked her if you'd treated her with kindness and respect. She said you had. I told her, me too. Said that was godly behavior, if anything was."

"Thank you."

"You bet. Didn't hurt that Winston got better after you were there."

"Just good luck," she breathed. It could have gone the other way. Sanne wasn't a miracle worker. Just a witch.

"Maybe so. but you've been a good neighbor," Johan said, "Helping when I needed it. Respecting the land. That's what counts. At least among those who matter. Anyone else, not worth your time."

Been a good neighbor. Past tense.

She swallowed. "Johan, don't sell your land."

"I tell you, I don't want to. But if the price is right..." he stared into the distance. "You don't know how much they're waving in front of me. It'd cover everything."

Sanne swallowed painfully.

"I know you love those old cedars, Susanne. Started paperwork to make them heritage. Protected. Just in case."

Just in case.

Gratitude flooded Sanne, but it wasn't enough to douse the sparks of dread eagerly looking for something to burn.

Sanne looked over Johan's house, fields, and the forest from which she had emerged. She could easily imagine a development here, all paved and carefully landscaped. A McMansion where Johan's house stood. Another there. The forest gone, replaced by asphalt, sidewalks, and manicured lawns.

Would a developer keep a patch of forest? Or even one tree? She imagined one great tree, lonely and ancient, caged by pavement, the last of its fellows.

No. They'd clearcut the whole thing, no matter what kind of designation Johan managed to get for the tree. They'd find a way.

"Coffee, Susanne?"

"Sure."

She met Johan's eyes, saw the weariness and grief there.

She must find a way, too.

FOUR

"W E ' V E   G O T   A   N E W   M E M B E R   I N   O U R   G R O U P today," Sanne told Angie and Rufus.

"Who?"

In the small town of Marigold, with two public middle schools and one private, there was a good chance that any two teens knew each other.

"New to town," Sanne said.

"Boy or girl?" Asked Rufus.

How to answer? "Wait and see," Sanne said.

"Hope it's a girl," Angie said. "Mom says we desperately need more women in computer science."

Angie, who was both female and Black, would have her work cut out for her in the still-white-male-dominated industry.

All the more reason for Sanne to make sure both of her charges were good at what they did, and ready to excel.

"Hell yeah, we need more women," added Rufus.

"Your parents good with that kind of language?" Sanne asked him pointedly.

"Sure. All I can't say is..."

"Nope, nope," Sanne cut in, shutting down the litany she was sure would follow. "Let's talk about Wikipedia and compression algorithms."

"Boring," Rufus sang.

"Think so? What if I told you data storage, retrieval, and compression are essential to artificial intelligence?"

"Oh!" Angie said, eyes alight. Then, "Ignore him."

Rufus nodded in agreement, eager to be ignored now that AI was on the table.

Sanne grinned and went to the whiteboard. She would draw a few pictures, talk a bit, and when the new teen arrived, clear the board and let Angie and Rufus teach instead. Getting kids to teach each other was one of the most effective ways of building understanding.

Good kids. Fun subject. She felt fortunate.

Images of the forest, of her grove of ancient trees, came to her, reminding her of how alive she felt to be with them.

She went to the board.

SANNE OPENED THE DOOR, INVITED KEYTON inside. Keyton, simply dressed in black, had short, curly hair, and gave a distance stare.

"My name's Keyton. My pronouns are ze and zir."

"What does that mean?" asked Rufus.

"It means ze isn't a boy or a girl," Angie answered. "Don't you watch stuff online?"

Rufus shook his head. "Nope. Not allowed. You—"

Rufus addressed Keyton. "You look like a girl with short hair."

Keyton's cheeks reddened. "Yeah? You look like a moron."

Angrily, Rufus stood. Keyton took a step toward him, chin high. Sanne smoothly stepped between them, a hand up toward each, subvocalizing a fast calming spell.

"None of that," she said aloud. "Keyton, have a seat. There, by Angie. And guess what, friends? This leads right into our next lesson."

It didn't, but teaching was all about being flexible.

Sanne went to the board, one eye on the kids, and began to draw rectangles.

"We've talked about binary digital computing. That's what your laptops run on. But what does that mean?"

Angie's hand shot up. Sanne nodded at her.

"When you go down to machine language, there's bits. They're ones or zeros."

"Gold star." Sanne wrote 0s and 1s in the rectangles. "But did you know that computers have used ternary logic for computing? That's three states, not just two." She wrote -1 in a couple of empty rectangles, paused to let that sink in. "Yet other computers use decimal digital computing— that's ten states per bit." She drew more numbers, and then looked at the teens.

Rufus was frowning. Angie was grinning. Keyton's cheeks were still red.

"Computing isn't just binary," Sanne added. "Any more than people are."

"Yeah," said Keyton adamantly.

"That's just weird," Rufus said.

"But it's right there in the silicon," Sanne replied, tapping the board with the marker. "The code you're learning lives on top of a base digital structure, so you don't know what's at the bit level, not really." She grinned at Keyton, who looked back suspiciously. "You'd have to ask the computer to be sure."

At this, Keyton nodded.

"Okay," Rufus said, clearly thinking it through. "So I'm male, Angie is female, and you—" this to Keyton. "You're what? Other?"

"Gender-fluid."

Before Rufus could make words from his confused expression, Sanne continued.

"And that leads us directly to the limitation of all this." Sanne waved her hand at the board. "Anyone want to take a guess?"

There was silence. After a long moment, Angie raised a tentative hand.

"Don't wait for permission, Ang. Just step in." Best to teach her early and often not to be too polite. Not in this field.

"It's still just one thing or another. Even decimal is only ten things. What about eleven? Or a hundred?"

"Angie's got a lock on the gold-star-feed today. It's all digital. So let's talk about analog. Like with game software."

"Yeah!" Rufus said, now keenly interested.

"The best joystick microprocessors are analog," Sanne continued. "A continuum rather than discrete states, because there's more than ten directions, right?" They all nodded. "Even subtle changes in direction matter when you're navigating."

"Totally matter." Rufus was fully engaged now. "You get a crap joystick with slop in it, you're screwed."

"Gotta be fluid," Keyton said pointedly.

"Exactly," Rufus said, giving zir a smile. He opened his laptop. "Let's get to work," he said officiously. "Want to leave time for knitting."

"Knitting?" Keyton did a double take, lost at this sudden change of topic.

"Or crochet," said Angie enthusiastically.

"Maybe better we don't today," Sanne said. "With Keyton just joining us—"

"Sanne teaches us how to weave things," Angie said, "if we get the assignment done fast enough. You're not the only strange one here," Angie said to Keyton in a reassuring tone. "We all are. Rufus is home-schooled. Mine is one of only five Black families in town. And Sanne is a witch."

Sanne felt shock course through her. "Uhm," she began.

"But along a continuum," added Rufus. "She's not a witch all the time, only when she's teaching us knitting."

"Or weaving herbs," added Angie.

"No," Sanne said forcefully, "No. That is not—" What was it not?

"You are a witch all the time?" Rufus asked with mock innocence.

Sanne stopped, stared back at the kids, realizing that she was on the defensive. How had that happened?

If this conversation made its way back to their parents, Rufus's especially, that might be the end of the group. Or worse—the end of her tutoring in this small town.

Then again, this witch stuff might have come directly

from their parents. How many people in Marigold were chatting about Sanne, if Donna Daley was telling the tale of Christmas eve and little Winston's recovery?

Wherever it came from, this was a delicate moment. Sanne licked her lips and gave each of them a short, focused look.

"A little history for you. In the Middle Ages, just accusing someone of being a witch could be enough to get them hanged. Or burned alive." She let that sink in. "People can call each other a lot of things, and some of them are pretty nasty, right?"

They nodded.

"For each person," Sanne continued, "could be a very different answer, when you ask them what they want to be called. Is that right?"

Angie nodded, a large motion. Keyton looked at the floor soberly.

Sanne met Rufus's look. "Rufus? Can I call you Roo-roo?"

Rufus's face scrunched. "No way."

"No way, indeed," Sanne said, and gave him a quick, reassuring smile.

"But we don't burn people anymore," Rufus said.

"Except maybe in games?"

"Oh, I see," he said. "Didn't think of that. Smooth. But they're not real, so it doesn't count."

How do you know what's real? Sanne didn't ask.

Sanne looked around the room, at bundles of hanging herbs, rocks of various colors and sizes, a jar of white sand, and the clear crystal her mother had given her for her tenth birthday, which was full of power and still held the slight etheric scent of her mother.

Sanne's gaze stopped at the red, orange, and green scarf hanging from her beat-up coat rack that started all this. She would not lie to them, but how she framed the truth was everything.

"You're right, Rufus," Sanne said. "These days, we don't burn people accused of witchcraft. But some people might not want their kids learning from people called witches, whether they are or not. It matters, the names we use for each other."

That landed. Angie looked alarmed. Keyton stared distantly.

Rufus looked straight at Sanne. "Okay, I get it," he said. "But are you?"

"Does it matter?" Sanne countered. "If I asked you to call me Susanne next week instead, would you still come to lessons?"

"Of course," he replied.

"There you go."

"Oh, I see," he said. In his expression Sanne saw that finally he did.

She had gotten lucky. Whether it was this generation, or these kids in particular, she read in their faces care, concern, and understanding.

Time to lighten things up.

"Do you guys know what the two hardest problems are in computer science?"

They all shook their heads.

"Cache invalidation, naming things, and off-by-one errors."

It took a few ticks of the analog clock before everyone laughed, the tension of the last few moments gone, like a morning fog blown away on a warm breeze.

"Moving on," Sanne said. "Rufus, Angie, you want to use the board and teach Keyton about storage, retrieval, and compression in AI? Show off what you know?"

They did.

FIVE

SANNE CUT OPEN THE BOX. JUST INSIDE WAS A note atop packing peanuts.

"I know your place is small," it read in Marla's neat handwriting, "but there's some weird stuff in here. Wasn't sure if it was trash or something valuable."

Weird stuff.

"Great," muttered Sanne, fishing through a sea of packing peanuts. Not the compostable sort, so they'd fill her small trash bucket.

Marla did not know just how small Sanne's place was, because Sanne hadn't exactly told her, or made her sister welcome here. Better to go to Marla's place with its guest room and extra bathrooms.

And lack of weirdnesses. It was too easy to imagine the look on Marla's face as she walked in the door of this one-room. Pained disappointment, it would be, just like Jerry's. Sanne could guess her thoughts: *My adult sister lives in one room? After all this time?*

Marla knew better than to offer Sanne money, and

Sanne knew better than to ask. Such money would come with pity and misunderstanding, and Sanne would rather live poor.

It wasn't the root of evil, the dollar, but it was surely the weedkiller of spirit. Whatever it touched, it bonded to, sequestered, and made inert. Money was the Jerry of the world.

Sanne smirked at this thought as she dug her hands into the sea of Styrofoam turds for what swam in the middle.

She tugged out a small, heavy wooden box, maybe a hand-length on the long side, brown and beat-up with decades of scratches and dents, and set it on the table.

No markings. No runes. No spells set upon the simple latch.

Even so, opening a box was like opening one's front door to someone—it always had the potential to let something in, or out, that you didn't expect.

Sanne eyed the new scarf on the coat rack. It was a clear-seeing spell, of a sort, but it came with a cost: sometimes you forgot what you thought you had known a moment before, washed away in the clarity of the moment.

Not just yet.

She clicked open the lid of the box and wrinkled her nose. The scent of musty earth wafted out along with a mustard-colored dust.

Decades old goldenseal, judging by the subdued scent and powdery condition. A common herb, good healing for various ills, dangerous for others, and now entirely useless. Likely something her mother had stored ages ago and forgotten about. Or died too soon to use.

Sanne herself had long ago resolved to not keep things

—it cluttered the space, the mind, and the spirit. Long ago, probably the very night flames had eaten her notebooks and spellbooks, an image that would never leave her.

It was best not to keep things that could be used against you if someone found them at the wrong time.

So Sanne took the box to the counter and slowly poured the inert dust into the sink, checking to be sure there wasn't anything else hidden there. One never knew, after all.

There wasn't.

She inspected the box. Thick and solid wood. It was almost big enough for knitting or crochet needles, if they were laid diagonally. Maybe one of the kids would want it.

Sanne's gaze panned the room, but her mind walked the forest. She didn't have much time. What could be done, now, to protect Johan's land?

It would need to be something more than a woven scarf, that was for sure.

SANNE WALKED THE BOUNDARIES OF JOHAN'S land, her scarf around her neck.

She had needed to memorize the plat map right there at the county offices, because despite the website saying copies could be bought, the woman there said they could not. The woman had also watched her closely as Sanne stifled her irritation and applied herself to putting the map directly into her visual memory.

It was a clear, crisp morning. Overhead, branches of

alder had begun to bud. Somewhere a finch trilled, a thrush beat bushes, and a squirrel chattered.

Sanne could lay a protection spell on the great trees, but that would pit her magic against the power of money, and that was a hard battle to win.

Battle was always costly. Better to start upstream. Divert the flow before it became a flood.

The first step of effective spellcasting was observation. You couldn't change the world until you understood how it was. If you wove a spell out of an imagined reality, as so many did, then nothing at all would shift.

The morning was cold enough that she was glad for the scarf, but it was long and unwieldy and she had to loop it twice. Still the tails dangled down to her knees.

With the scarf's spell around her neck and shoulders, sound and scent changed subtly. Birdsong was barely affected, but human sounds, like the distant buzz of a chainsaw, or a car on the highway, came into sharper focus.

The wind shifted, and sounds changed. She heard the creak of high branches, the determined shrill of a hawk, and her own footsteps soft along the dirt road that clung to the border of Johan's land.

Sometimes spells were no more than wishful thinking. You might cast, weave, or lay a spell, believing the outcome was the result of your own work, when actually it was random chance.

One must be in the right mindset to understand cause and effect. One must always be on guard against superstition and self-delusion.

But self-delusion could be used effectively against others who were not on guard against it.

Sanne crouched. Here, according to the map in her memory, was where the boundary of Johan's land angled past the road into the brush beyond. It was a corner of the property, and as such had potential for border magic.

She dug into the soft, rich dirt with a stick. When the narrow hole was a half-foot or so deep, she took one of the charms she'd made from sage, wild ginger, saskatoon berry, and duckfoot, along with a pinch of fireweed pollen. She inserted the charm into the hole and spoke a spell as she packed the dirt again, then covered it with leaves.

The charm was a seed that would grow an illusion.

With the scarf on, the ground where the charm was buried glowed then faded. She unlooped the scarf and looked again.

The land seemed plain. Of little value. Not worth a second glance. She relooped the scarf and continued her walk, planting seed-charms into the afternoon.

It was a good start.

Walking back, she passed the apple trees in Johan's front yard, their flowers still fists, the fingers slowly uncurling. That so many of them looked like middle-finger signs facing the road made her smile.

Who were they, the agents Johan had been talking with? What were they about?

What did they want?

CHAPTER

SIX

Della narrowed her eyes at Terry. He was snapping his gum loudly. In the years they'd been somewhat more than business partners, she had become convinced he did it only to annoy her.

Della was responsible for making and keeping their shared fortune. He admired her success, but he didn't understand it.

It didn't matter. He was a pretty man. He kept himself in shape, had a nicely formed chin, and knew how to use those bedroom eyes that were like warm pools of water.

He unrolled the plat diagrams on the desk between them.

"Ninety-seven-point-eight acres," Della said, tracing the outline of the property with a pink-lacquered fingernail. "LR5. Modern sewer connect. No disputed or messy easements. I like it. The developers will, too."

"If MacKenzie sells," Terry replied.

Not a question, but it should have been. The truth was that Terry had no idea how to get people to sell.

That was Della's work.

Terry turned from the desk, aiming his head at the trash can, and spat gum across the room like a missile. It landed with a hard thunk in the can.

"Yes!" he said, triumphantly.

"Grow up."

He grinned at her. "How much is it worth to you, darlin'? A thousand a piece?"

"You've got one more month of chewing that shit, and then you'll stop," Della said, turning her attention back to the plat drawings.

"Sure I will." He followed her gaze to the map. "MacKenzie stands to become a very rich man, if we pay him even close to market. What do you think he'll take?"

"We'll offer him better than market."

Terry's look at her was sharp. "We'll what?"

Della considered the numerous developers she knew, who knew her. She ranked them in her head, according to several factors. Flexibility. Reliability. Money.

"Developers A, B, and C are going to cream over this," Della said. "A bidding war, if we play our cards right. But getting MacKenzie on contract will take more than money."

"What more?"

"He's recently applied for three heritage tree designations."

"Oh." A long sound. "Your friend Lisa, at the county office. Still owes you?"

"Still." Lisa needed emotional reassurance, now and then. Sometimes desperately. Della provided.

Terry cocked his head. "Will he get his trees?"

Della gave an exaggerated shrug, her tone amused. "The county moves so slowly these days. I expect MacKenzie will have to make a decision on our offer long before the county even notices those applications."

Terry's look was sober. "You're talking a hell of a lot of money, Della."

"It's only money." She enjoyed saying that, because of how visibly uncomfortable it made Terry. But she wasn't serious; money was Della's forte, how it worked, how it flowed, and how to get more. "We need to do a little prep. We need to know what MacKenzie wants, and how to make sure he doesn't get it."

"Except from us."

"Except from us," she echoed, handing Terry a flip pad of paper. "Find all this out for me, darlin'. Paper only."

Terry snorted at being told what to do, but didn't object. An obedient sort, mostly. As long as she kept him feeling secure.

As he glanced at Della's instructions, he asked, "What will you be doing, darlin' o' mine?"

"I'll be making sure no stone is left unturned."

He frowned. "Why would you want to turn a stone? Oh, you mean you're on the hunt."

She leaned across the desk and stroked his handsome chin. Not that clever, her Terry. But she didn't need him to be.

Her phone chimed, and from the sound of the ring, Della knew there was money behind it. One of her developers, no doubt.

They knew her by name, now. Knew her reputation.

How she could get reluctant owners to sign over prime pieces of developable land.

She smiled and took the call.

TERRY'S MIND WAS ON DIAMONDS.

A diamond would do it, if it were large enough.

That was the thought circling through his mind when the white Huskie pup slipped its owner's hold and ran full speed onto Main street, right in front of Terry's car.

He realized that something had happened, but a blink too late.

Visions of diamonds, of the rings he could only afford because Della was so damned good at what she did, cleared from his mind, replaced by a small flash of white that was now somewhere under his car.

Terry slammed on the brakes, came to a stop.

He threw open the car door, but for a moment couldn't move from the seat. A young woman with teal-tinted hair was in front of his car, yelling, "Poppy! Poppy!" She bent over, calling again.

Terry stumbled from the car. He could barely feel his feet. Breath came short and shallow, as if he'd been running. He stood, hand on the car door, unmoving.

He battled the images flooding his mind, telling himself that he never saw it, that he was being weak, foolish, emotional. All the things Della hated.

She'd never marry him, not like this. He had to be strong. Smooth.

He'd smile reassuringly at the teal-haired woman, tell

her not to worry. He'd bend over and pick up Poppy the puppy, trembling but intact, and hand the cute little bugger to the woman. The gathered crowd would applaud as the teal-haired woman smiled, gratefully, tearfully, taking her puppy into her arms.

Terry the hero. Not Terry the monster who ran over a young woman's puppy in front of the entire town.

Della would never forgive him. Not the puppy—she wouldn't care—but the scene it caused, the taint to her reputation as a caring real estate broker in a small town where reputation was everything.

Puppy killer. He could already hear it being whispered behind his back.

There would be blood on the pavement.

No, dammit, that was memory.

He willed himself to breathe, to move. To take a step. Just one.

Blood on the pavement.

Not his fault. He had seen the girl playing moments before, smirked at how stupid she was to be putting toy soldiers behind the wheels of the white SUV, wondering whether she'd turn into a general someday, or maybe, with that kind of intelligence, just be a burger flipper.

Those were the thoughts of his fourteen-year old self, next door, in his own yard. Big for his age, attractive and charming. He knew he was better than she was.

He had looked away, following the trail of a hawk in the air. Red tail or Peregrine from the way it was hovering, he thought, and he mused on hunting and killing and what it would be like to fly. He barely noticed the sound of a car starting up, nothing unusual in this suburban neighborhood.

But then the odd sound. The crunch. He had turned to look.

A white car door, a woman's voice. There was screaming and more screaming, then crying over a small crumpled figure.

When it was all done and over and everything had been moved, there was blood on the pavement.

Days later Terry found a small, crushed plastic soldier at the edge of the grass where it had happened. By then, someone had cleaned the pavement, but Terry crouched down close to inspect, that day and many days following, and at the edge, where grass met asphalt, he could always find a bit of blood.

It wasn't his fault.

"Poppy!" The teal-haired woman was calling.

In a moment, Terry knew, she'd start to scream and cry, because that's how it would go. But this time Terry was a man. He couldn't say he hadn't heard the car. Hadn't seen anything.

As he stood there immobile, a small sound escaped, a tiny sound, like breath, or the smallest of pleading whines. The sort a dog in pain might make.

He just needed to move. He'd go find Poppy the puppy and it would be all right.

Terry's eyes were blurring. He saw motion, a teal head bobbing up and down at the front of his car.

"Little idiot," muttered someone close by.

Terry turned his head. Next to him stood the hardware

guy, in his faded Metallica T-shirt and apron caked with sawdust.

"Entitled little bitch," said the man, just soft enough for Terry to hear. "And no, I don't mean the dog." He snorted at his own humor. "Keep it on a leash, this wouldn't happen."

For a moment, Terry was completely lost. You couldn't keep a child on a leash. Weren't there laws about that?

Out of the corner of his eye, the teal-haired woman held a bundle. A small bundle covered in blood.

Terry felt sick.

"I didn't mean to," Terry whispered, still staring at the hardware guy.

The man looked back, his expression changing. "You okay, buddy?"

"Fine."

"Don't worry about it," the hardware guy said. "Not your fault."

His mother had said the same thing. The words meant nothing.

The sickness inside him threatened to come out of his throat. His stomach heaved. He clenched down.

Not your fault.

Terry forced his head to turn, forced and forced, but it moved slowly, so slowly, like a broken machine. At last he stared at the front of his car, where the teal-haired woman stood, with a bloody, lifeless bundle in her arms.

A handful of townspeople huddled around her. They were all smiling.

Smiling?

Terry blinked, cleared his eyes. Blinked again.

No blood. In her arms, little Poppy was licking the woman's face, tail enthusiastically beating her arm.

No blood.

For a moment, Terry wondered if there was something wrong with him.

As Terry's heart thudded, the street began to clear. The teal-haired waved at him, her expression grateful as if he had done something good, rather than almost hit her dog. The hardware guy patted his shoulder in a gesture of camaraderie.

In moments, the street was empty. When he could move, Terry got back in his car and started the engine.

Della would need a very large diamond. He had to convince her that he was serious, that he was worth the trouble to marry.

Very large. Nothing else would do.

CHAPTER

SEVEN

IT WASN'T THAT SHE WAS LAZY, SANNE EXPLAINED to herself as she put on shoes and grabbed her backpack, eyeing the clock to be sure she had time.

It was simply that as long as there was food in the house, it seemed silly to go through the trouble to get more. Yes, that meant that she often opened cans, and one could get tired of black beans and salt, but... it was still food.

But now she was out of coffee, and that was a problem.

She quickly checked her debit card balance. Yes, she could still afford coffee.

Sanne had been reluctant to spend money on a new coffee maker after the old one died despite her best attempts to magic it to keep going. The new one was due soon. Could be today.

She walked to the Marigold grocery, collecting things into her basket, and heading toward the eggs. The aisle before her was half-obstructed by an unattended dolly of soup cans. The labels on the cans were yellow-orange, about the same shade as an egg yolk.

That caught her attention long enough to see a pattern across the cans, one that resembled a runic symbol that meant *pay attention.*

Sanne stared. The difference between coincidence and the world passing along useful information to those who could see it was a razor-thin business.

More likely, she was reading too much into soup can labels.

Gathering the rest of what she had come for, she paid, slung the backpack full of groceries over her shoulders, and left the store.

A quick walk home, with a short detour, was what she had in mind. But with the maybe-message of the soup cans, she decided to pause a moment and look around.

Across the street, a hardware store. A diner. A pet supply. The thrift-antique store where Sanne got most of her clothes. At the far end of the street, a firehouse, the park, and the old dance hall.

It was a typical spring Saturday. Families wandered, shopping. A farmer and a home-repair enthusiast came out of the hardware store, chatting. A teal-haired young woman stepped out of the thrift store, jangling the bells on the handle, a white bundle in her arms.

Nothing out of the ordinary.

Sanne turned, walked to the next building and stopped.

A swirl of odd energy came to awareness. A tiny, subtle thing, like a breeze, dismissible in the general chaos of the human field.

Turning in place, senses alert, she felt into the world around her to find the source, up and down the street, rising to the second stories of buildings, dipping into the basements.

From up the street came a growling sound, a car with a powerful engine driving just a bit too fast.

Then, across the street, the teal-haired woman put her bundle on the ground, a leash in her other hand, ready to clip onto the collar of a puppy, bouncing excitedly. Before she could secure it, it dashed into the street, on a collision course with a blue car.

The car would win.

Sanne didn't think. She expanded her full field across the scene. She made a hard bubble.

One.

Sanne dropped the center of her energy deep into the earth, far below the sidewalk, to establish a solid ground.

Two.

Sanne slowed time.

Three.

Foolish, she would later tell herself. What had she been thinking? Might as well have rung the old firehouse bell. To anyone able to hear, this kind of magic was like a fire alarm.

In the moment, Sanne thought no such thing. She acted. Into this instant of time she slid another one, and into that a third, like doors containing doors, pockets within pockets.

She gave the puppy a second to glance around, to see the approaching tires. He considered one direction, then the other, then stepped between them.

Once there, Sanne held him secure.

Then she released the moment. Time returned to normal.

A woman's cry. A man's shout. A car coming to an abrupt stop.

Everyone turned to look.

The driver got out of the blue car. The teal-haired woman ran into the street. Others followed. The driver stood like a statue, hand on his car door, the only unmoving figure as everyone swirled around him.

The woman bent over, picked up the small white creature, cradled it in her arms. People surrounded her, gathering to touch the puppy, who was happy for the attention. Reassuring words were exchanged, relieved laughter filled the air.

At last, the driver slowly got back into his car, hunched, as if he himself had been hit.

Sanne gaped. That's what had originally caught her attention, this man. He was wrapped in various powerful enchantments, like sticky webs of colors that didn't exist in nature.

Only now did she also realize that she recognized him: he was the man in the intensely pink sportscar at Johan's place, alongside the woman at the wheel. The real estate agents.

Sanne had lived in Marigold for many years. It was a small town and she knew nearly everyone. Certainly anyone who dabbled in the crafting of spells, whether they knew it or not.

There was no one in Marigold who could cast that sort of enchantment.

Who were they?

∼

Sᴀɴɴᴇ's ᴅᴇᴛᴏᴜʀ ᴛᴏᴏᴋ ʜᴇʀ ᴛᴏ ᴏɴᴇ ᴏғ ᴛʜᴇ town's two small real estate storefronts.

She knew the man who worked there by sight. He smiled and gestured her inside.

"Sure, I know those two," he said when Sanne described the cars and the couple she had seen. "You're talking about Della Meyer and Terrance Hundley. Moved to town a few months back."

"Moved here?"

"Right as rain. Looking at the old Polla place and also Mr. MacKenzie's. Large parcels, ideally, but said they're open to residential. Especially larger corner lots. Got something?"

Sanne forced an amused laugh. "Not me."

"Well, keep them in mind if you hear of something. Got a card somewhere." He opened a drawer. "Here." He handed her a card of heavy stock, embossed, and gold edged.

Old-school glitz, intended to impress people of an older generation. Like Johan.

No coincidence that Mr. Hundley had been driving through town just now. He lived here.

Sanne said her goodbyes and hurried home.

The kids were due for a lesson this afternoon. She put the mystery of the real estate agent couple aside while she thought about what her students would be studying today.

CHAPTER

EIGHT

DELLA STOOD AT THE WINDOW OF HER penthouse, one of the few tall buildings in Marigold, only recently completed under the new zoning. She stared.

Someone had changed the cadence of time.

Della could see the quaint downtown, the now-decorative firehouse belltower. Distantly, hills and farms, many of them derelict.

Unused. Wasted land. Which was why she was here.

Just a few minutes ago Della had felt the ripples from the brief time change. She came to the window. It seemed to emanate from the center of Marigold. It was powerful magic.

She stood minutes more as it dissipated, then turned her back on the window, staring unseeing at the prints on her walls, the straight lines of buildings she had helped to bring into existence, the grand white colonial porch of the Crestor development she'd most recently shepherded through.

In this small town was someone with the power to slow

time. Even a large city rarely boasted such a worker. A surprise, to be certain.

But as long as whoever it was didn't get in Della's way, it didn't matter. Better they didn't cross paths.

Making money was one of Della's greatest pleasures, and it lent itself, conveniently, to making more. Her second greatest pleasure was buying whatever she wanted, whenever she wanted it. She was careful to always hold in mind a thing just beyond her capacity, something more costly than she could yet afford.

Her gaze sought and found the last picture on the wall, a glorious and magnificent Azimut 72 motor yacht. Silver. She would have it tricked out in pale lavender with ivory leather interior.

It was also deliciously out of reach. But if the properties she had her sights on fell into line and into place, leading to happy developers, she'd be able to order that exquisite dream yacht.

And that would be a good day.

Della had come to Marigold for the many opportunities that new zoning and failing rural economies provided. She'd made a good chunk of cash in Pine Bluff, Montana. When it was done, she had made a few enemies, but that was to be expected. Now, she had enough to make more serious plays, like the MacKenzie and Polla lands.

There hadn't been much resistance in Pine Bluff. She'd come in with a bunch of cash, offered extras to ease the way of a retiring old cattle rancher, and had made a small fortune. People everywhere were easy to steer, with the right combination of cash and spellcraft.

That small fortune had also bought her a Tesla model S,

in her favorite shade of dark bubblegum. Every time she drove it, she felt herself thrum with life.

Less so when she occasionally had to drive Terry's royal blue Mustang, overpowered and loud. A bit like Terry.

Speaking of...she checked her phone's tracking app. Where was he and what was he up to?

He was just passing a mall south of downtown. Probably just missed the time-change magic, whatever it was. Wouldn't have been able to feel it, even if he had been in the middle of it when it happened. He was not a worker.

And now? At the mall, no doubt buying himself some new toy. His room was littered with such objects, from model trains to die-cast classic cars to remote-control helicopters. She liked to tease him that if he played his cards right, someday he could have the real thing.

He would smile, but it would be weak. He was, she suspected, jealous of the fact that she was the one making the big deals. She drove the partnership, it was true, but they would go to the next level together.

Della had come to Marigold with cash in pocket, a plan, and every reason to believe that the town would be as easy to seduce as a kitten charmed by a bit of string.

A grin came over her face. The more she thought about it, the more she liked the idea that the kitten might have claws, and be a bit of a challenge to subdue.

Not too much. Just enough to be amusing.

NINE

Sanne tossed cans into cabinets, swearing she'd organize them later. She slid the eggs and milk into her small fridge and cleared the table mostly into the sink. She looked around for any other stray, attractive nuisances.

With that thought, she snatched the long scarf from the coat rack and stuffed it under her bed, which was already a storm of pillows and sheets. A fast snap of the blanket and it was all covered.

With a rag, she cleared the worst of the bits of plant and flower that had fallen to the floor from the drying rack.

One of the upsides of teaching in her own home was that it forced her to straighten up, necessarily countering her own sloppy tendencies.

There, that would do. The room was at least passable. For kid company.

A knock. Sanne grinned—she could tell from the cadence whose it was.

She opened the door to Rufus, immediately followed by a panting Keyton who had likely sprinted from the bus stop a few blocks away. They stormed in and began to set up their laptops on the table.

A moment later Angie arrived. She held a twig of green.

"This good for something?" she asked.

Sanne grinned at the fat green needles. "Rosemary. Get that from the parkway down the block?"

Angie nodded.

"It removes worry. Helps get you good grades."

Rufus and Keyton looked attentively.

"Really?" asked Angie.

"Well," Sanne said, "you also have to study."

"Ha!" Rufus said.

"We think you should teach us wildcrafting," Keyton said.

"Do you? I'll wait until I hear that from your parents," Sanne said, moving to the whiteboard. "All right, my friends. It's time to talk about the internet and TCP/IP packets. What, you might wonder—"

"We didn't," Rufus said.

"—is TCP? Or IP, for that matter?" Sanne continued.

"Intellectual property," replied Keyton. "Like Bart Simpson."

"Or SpongeBob."

"Or Pete the Cat."

"Yes, to all that," Sanne said, suppressing a smile at these clever retorts. "But also it means Internet Protocol, which has everything to do with—"

Another knock at the door, this one with business-like staccato. Sanne hesitated. It repeated.

She opened the door to find a large box at her feet and a man with a tablet.

"Susanne Pascrel"?

"Yes?"

He gestured at the box. "For you. This—" He held up a large, full-sized, cardboard envelope. "Needs a signature."

"Bring in the box for you?" asked Keyton helpfully from just behind her.

"Sure. Thanks. Careful—it's my new coffee maker," Sanne said.

The kids snaked around her eagerly, carting the large box inside. She heard Rufus whisper: "See? She was just talking about packages! I told you."

"Packets," corrected Angie.

"What's this?" Sanne asked, of the envelope he was holding.

The postman shrugged. "Probably important. Tracked to within an inch of its life."

On the envelope was Marla's return address.

Sanne sighed, and signed on the tablet where the man indicated. She thanked him and accepted the envelope, which felt heavier than it was. The postman wished her a good day. Sanne retreated back inside.

"Should we open the box for you, Sanne?" asked Angie, who had found scissors.

"Sure," Sanne answered, as she wrestled with the envelope, finally finding the fancy pull-tab to open. Within this one was another envelope.

What could Marla have thought so important it needed tracking?

Within the second thick envelope, which included a third, Sanne found a note in Marla's handwriting.

Dear sister: Jerry wrote this for you before he passed. He asked me to make sure you got it. I hope you'll read it. Love always.

A complex tangle of emotions came over Sanne, starting with anger.

There was nothing Jerry could say to her now, nothing she wanted to hear from him, and Marla would know this. Sanne set the envelope atop the bookshelf. Her sister could have saved herself the trouble by asking Sanne, and Sanne would have told her to burn the damned thing, fitting end to Jerry's last words to her. Marla knew Sanne would not want something anything from Jerry, but she'd sent it anyway.

"Wow, check this out!" said Rufus. "Smooth!"

Sanne looked. The kids had opened the packing box, finding another box within—boxes in boxes seemed to be Marla's preferred method—and were now holding a third one.

Styrofoam turds covered the table and much of the floor. Rufus held the third box, about a foot deep and half again as long. It was wrapped in aging butcher paper, and tied quite thoroughly with brown packing twine.

With the box, Rufus pushed the table clear, sending the other boxes and the rest of the packing peanuts onto the floor.

Sanne made an annoyed sound. "Hey. You'll all help me clean this up, right, guys?"

"We will," Keyton promised. Angie nodded.

The three kids gathered around the third box. Sanne was just thinking that it seemed a bit small for a coffee maker, when Angie cut the strings.

Sanne felt a spell spark to life. She closed the distance to them fast.

A ward, a repellent, a warning. It came tinged with her mother's etheric scent.

On the brown paper were two words, written long ago in faded red marker, in her mother's hand, in a private language they shared, that Sanne had not seen in years.

"What's it say, Sanne?"

The butcher paper, now untied, curled open on its own, hiding the two words.

Many things flashed through Sanne's mind at once.

First, the ward wasn't working on the kids. It had aged and weakened, perhaps. More likely, it was not tuned to this time and place, made, as it was, decades ago, in another land.

Second, the words read: *Demon eggs.*

Her sister had sent her demon eggs. Marla could not possibly know what the words said, and wouldn't believe it even if she had.

Sanne was stunned: she had no idea her mother had such a thing, let alone more than one. Demon eggs were rare beyond rare. Her mother had never even mentioned them; Sanne had learned about them by studying.

Demon eggs. Holy crap.

"It's junk," Sanne said, struggling to seem unmoved. "From an old relative."

The paper continued to slowly curl back. The kids didn't seem to notice that strangeness. Then cardboard flaps, unbound, cracked open and began to rise.

"I like junk," Angie said innocently, her hands diving

into the box, where ancient cotton batting was the first layer. "Can we see?"

"No. Leave it," Sanne said, her tone hard and edged. "We have lessons to get to."

Angie pulled back as if stung.

"About packages, yeah, we know," said Rufus flatly. "But I want to know what's inside this one."

Keyton grinned. "This particular packet starts with three nested boxes and ends with...well, we don't know yet."

"Is the writing the checksum?" Rufus asked the other two.

"Can't be," Angie replied. "Because we're the reader, and we can't read it. So it's got to be content."

"Maybe it's not directed at us," suggested Keyton. "Maybe we're actually sniffer malware."

"Fully authorized," Angie said primly. "Packet was sent to Sanne, who delegated it to us to open."

Despite Sanne's alarm, she was charmed to see that they'd read the material. "Well done," Sanne said. "But let's get back to—"

"You said it was junk," Rufus said stubbornly. "That means you don't care what it is. So let us see."

"Please, Sanne?" Keyton asked.

According to everything Sanne had read, the eggs shouldn't look special. Every authoritative text assured the reader that demons hid in the guise of something quite plain. The eggs even more so. It was how they survived in the world.

Demon magic. Powerful magic.

The last thing she needed was for them to know what it

was. Sanne should be able to show what was inside to the kids, pack it again, and figure out what to do with it after they left.

They were watching her. Angie hopeful, Keyton fascinated, and Rufus...suspicious.

He was used to adults lying to him, she realized. Until now, Sanne had never.

"Okay," she said, resolving to show herself to be trustworthy. "Let me. Just in case it's—" what? "—sharp."

As Sanne put her hands into the batting, she dissipated the rest of the ward. A sharp pang of sorrow accompanied the fleeting sense of her mother's handiwork.

Judging by the age of the batting, and the old scent of the paper, this might have been packed before Sanne was even born. Marla had found it. Not knowing what it was, thinking Sanne might find it precious, she had packed it and sent it on.

A kind of respect, now that Sanne thought about it. Marla didn't believe any of what Sanne did. Even so, she honored her sister's path in the world. That was love, wasn't it?

Yes, it was.

Sanne set the first layer of discolored off-white batting on the table, and went back for the next layer. Her fingers brushed something hard underneath. She pulled off the next layer and saw green.

Three eggs, side by side, each some four inches in length, and the color of unripe avocados.

"Wow. What are those?" asked Rufus.

"Pretty," said Keyton.

To Sanne's horror, Angie's hand darted forward and brushed one of the eggs with a finger.

"Emu eggs," Angie answered. "And they're not empty."

"Let's not touch them," Sanne said quickly.

Angie obediently withdrew her hand.

"Emu eggs?" Sanne asked her.

"Sure," Angie said. "My aunt works at a farm. I've been in with the big birds, even. Seen them lay. These ones, from the color, are just laid."

"Wow!" said Rufus.

"But I don't get it," Angie said. "Why would someone send you fresh emu eggs?"

Sanne knew they weren't. They were decades old. Maybe older.

And these were hardly plain things. Had the lore she'd read been wrong?

"Okay. We've seen them," she said, forcing a grin, as she replaced the cotton batting. "Let's get back to—"

"Three!" Rufus cried delightedly. "One for each of us. Smooth!"

"No, no, no," Sanne said, in what she hoped was a calm yet firm manner. "Not for you. But the lesson is."

Rufus's expression went hard. "You said they were junk."

"I did."

"You didn't know what was in the package," he said accusingly.

Keyton tilted zir head at Sanne. "Yeah, you looked surprised. But you said it was junk, like you knew what it was. So..."

"So it's none of our business," Angie said firmly to the other two. "Sanne has a right to her privacy."

"Thank you," Sanne said gratefully.

But there was doubt in Rufus and Keyton's faces, and that was no good. The depth of the kids' trust was what allowed her to teach them so quickly and effectively. It was what made the kids want to come back. That kept the kids happy, Sanne happy, and the parents happy. That was why she got paid.

Any hint of deception would undercut it all. Even if the kids never found out, they would feel it, just below the surface, the disconnect between words and actions.

However, she could not tell them. You couldn't expect a thirteen-year-old to keep secrets like this one, something this outrageous. Could hardly expect an adult to, either.

It was dangerous knowledge.

"I thought it was something else," Sanne said carefully, holding their attention. And that was true—it looked nothing like the coffee maker she had been expecting. She took a breath and let it out slowly, exhaling a silent, soft spell, to clear the air between them. "I was wrong. It's not junk. It's from my sister. I don't quite know what to do with it yet."

All true.

She saw their shoulders relax, their expressions ease.

"Well," said Angie, "you could eat them."

"Eat them?" Rufus asked her, fascinated.

"Will they hatch?" Keyton asked.

Angie shrugged. "If they're fertile and incubated, maybe. But these aren't being kept warm, so I don't think so."

Dread came over Sanne. *If they're fertile.*

Of course they were fertile. They were demon eggs.

And she was sure that they wouldn't need any kind of special treatment to incubate. She briefly touched the middle one, feeling for a spark of life. Nothing.

Well-hidden.

"How long do they incubate?" Sanne asked with dread.

"About a month and a half, I think," Angie said.

"You can eat them?" Rufus asked Angie again.

"Yeah. If they're not rotten."

"But how?"

"Break it open. Like a regular egg."

"A really, really big egg," Keyton added.

"Oh, let's make a scrambled egg!" said Rufus delightedly.

"Nope, nope, and more nope," Sanne answered. "We need to get back to the lesson."

She watched their faces. Their imaginations had been sparked, and that was good. They were no longer wondering if she were lying to them, and that was even better.

But how to steer their attention? How to get back to a lesson when strange eggs were just sitting here? Talk about attractive nuisances.

"The fundamental problem with the internet," Sanne said. "Anyone?"

"It exists, my dad says," said Rufus.

"It's a mess, my mom says," Angie replied.

"Both right," Sanne said, grinning. "And Keyton was right, too, asking about sniffer malware."

Sanne took a step away from the eggs, and they stepped with her. Then another. They followed.

"Sniffer-ware is easy to make, it turns out," Sanne said.

"Really?" Keyton asked.

"Really. The internet was designed for reliability, not security. So packets of content, which we've been studying..." She went to the sink, held up a dirty dish for them to see. "This dish is content. You can see what's inside it, easy. But if you encrypt it..." she nodded at the eggs. "You have no idea what's inside."

"But we could break the shell and see," Rufus said.

Sanne suppressed a shudder.

"You could try. There are various kinds of encryption." Sanne walked back to the table with the laptops. The kids followed. "How about this: I'll tell you how to identify a weak encryption, and break it. Then I'll tell you about a guy who would bounce on a mini-trampoline while he talked, who invented the most unbreakable encryption algorithm ever, and why you can't break it. Yet."

They were intrigued. A trace of suspicion remained on Rufus's face.

There was still a weight in the room. They weren't quite ready.

"So," she asked them. "Want to hear a TCP joke?"

"Sure," Rufus replied. The other two nodded.

"Okay," Sanne said, "I'll tell you a TCP joke." She waited.

"Yeah?" Keyton prompted at last.

Sanne nodded decisively. "I'm about to send the TCP joke. It'll last 10 seconds, has three characters, no setting, and ends with a punchline."

Angie was already snickering. "Okay," Angie said. I'm ready to hear your joke, which is 10 seconds, three characters, no setting, and ends with a punchline."

Sanne could tell from Rufus and Keyton's expressions that they almost understood. It was a slow dawning. She waited a moment more.

Timing was everything.

"I'm sorry," Sanne said with a wider grin. "Your connection has timed out." She gave them all a look. "Do you want to hear a TCP joke?"

Laughter was great magic, and fine medicine.

Now, they were ready.

CHAPTER

TEN

Della nodded politely at Vikie Williams, director of Lakeview Terrace Assisted Living and Memory Care. Vikie led them forward, continuing to point out various features of the facility: gardens, soft walking paths, and game night.

But Della's attention was elsewhere. She was checking off her mental list.

A surprise sewer and gas inspection for the MacKenzie property would show numerous violations. Even if the inspectors were mistaken, which was likely, the reports would necessitate more inspections. Someone would doubtless mention to Mr. MacKenzie just how expensive fixing all that would be.

A neighbor would come forward, convinced that a decades-old question about property lines should be resurrected, and that there was no point in talking with MacKenzie about it. Better to take it to the courts.

Finally, a question had come to the county's attention about buried tanks on the property and whether they had been legally decommissioned or not, a question that would need to be answered.

Johan MacKenzie would soon be busy with expensive problems that Della could help solve.

The tour completed, Della sat in a small office across from Vikie Williams, who placed a glossy brochure and forms in front of her.

Never cheap, assisted living. Lakeview was high-end.

But Johan MacKenzie wouldn't need to know how much it cost, not until he had signed the contract.

"I'll be blunt, Vickie," Della said. "I've visited every other facility within an hour of Marigold." She hadn't, but she'd called them all, and made sure they understood. "You're the best."

Della put power into the words, power tuned to the particulars of the woman across from her.

A vulnerable, childlike expression broke through Vikie's professional smile. Her voice wavered. "Thank you. Do you think your friend's father might be happy here?"

"Quite confident of it." Della tapped a long, pale pink nail on the paperwork. "As it happens, I'm a bit of a philanthropist."

Vikie blinked at this sudden change of direction. "Oh?"

"You have how many openings at Lakeview?"

"Two. We've a wait-list as well."

Vikie pulled out her phone. "I would so love to give this fine institution the confidence that it can continue to serve its clientele at this superb level of care. May I make a donation?"

"A donation?" Vikie asked, bemused.

With effort Della suppressed a smile, seeking instead for

a most sincere expression. Lakeview wasn't accustomed to getting donations from complete strangers.

Della thumbed her phone. "I've taken the liberty of identifying your routing number, and—there. I've deposited ten K into your account for you to use as you see fit."

Della enjoyed moments like these. Nothing was better than spending small money that would lead to big money.

"Ten thousand?" Vikie mouthed.

"How much to hold both those spots, in case my friend's father likes one better than the other?"

"Ah," Vikie said. "We don't usually…"

"Of course you don't," Della said, but by now, Della's exact words didn't matter. She was working a deep spell on Vikie as she thumbed her phone again. "I know you'd be happy to, in my rather unusual situation. There." She looked at the other woman. "I've transferred another ten K, and will do so monthly until we have finalized a decision with your fine organization."

Vikie's eyes went wide, as if Della were offering a grand Christmas present.

"All I ask of you, my dear," Della continued, "is that you make it clear to anyone inquiring that there are now no openings at Lakeview Terrace, and the wait-list is full. But you'll hold my spot. Will you do that for me?"

"Of course." Vikie's tone, expression, and forward-leaning posture said that she would do anything for Della.

Money and magic could get just about anything done.

Della stood, took Vikie's hand affectionately, holding it a moment longer, affectionately, to build a sustaining etheric channel.

Della knew that Johan MacKenzie, after he sold his property to Della, would stay in Marigold. He had a church. Lifelong friends. He'd want his parents close by.

The elder MacKenzie would need to be in a home, and soon. One that could handle memory and cognition problems. That was expensive care, and Johan MacKenzie would finally be able to afford it.

But if he went looking for it, he would find that there were no openings anywhere. Only the ones that Della controlled.

Sealing a deal was all about setting things in motion in advance. Arranging the board. Once you did that, the final, signed contract was really rather trivial. Like dropping the last ball into the pocket with a light tap.

Della sat in her Tesla, appreciating its delicious purr, and let herself smile.

CHAPTER

ELEVEN

After the lesson, good to their word, the kids helped collect packing peanuts into the trash and went home.

Sanne stared at the big empty packing boxes and mulled over her lengthening list of troubles.

Johan possibly selling his land. Her grove of trees and their safety. These agents, Della Meyer and Terrance Hundley, one of whom was wearing enchantments.

Demon eggs on her table.

There was no reason, she realized with increasing dread, that these eggs would have the same incubation period as the emu eggs they pretended to be.

How long did it take demon eggs to hatch? Was there a triggering event? Had it already happened?

Sanne needed to know more.

She took the scissors to cut open the flaps of the larger packing boxes so she could flatten them and set them out for recycling.

She froze.

On the scissors was a trace of ancient magic, one that had not been there before, like a residue of oil on a previously clean tool.

She gingerly touched the scissor blades with her forefinger, trying to understand the origin and nature of the spell. It faded and was gone.

Her gaze panned the room. The cut twine was coiled under a cabinet toe-kick. She picked it up. The string tasted of the same magic, dark and old. It, too, dissipated.

Not her mother's work. Something older.

If the eggs were sensitive, what had Angie done by touching one? What had Sanne begun by touching another?

She let out a long stream of air. Johan's land. The trees. Important.

But preventing demons from hatching out in the small town of Marigold? More important.

After her uncle Jerry had fed her irreplaceable library to the flames, a teenaged Sanne had learned to hide her books. Under floorboards. Tucked into attic insulation.

On a shelf with other books, under false covers.

She'd learned to enchant her books, to make them seem dull and tedious at a glance. That didn't work on Jerry, always alert for Sanne's strangeness, and having his own anti-magic twist, even if he didn't believe it. But it allowed Sanne to store her books at the school library, in the open.

Then it occurred to Sanne that if she could make books seem as if they weren't interesting to other people, maybe other witches who had come before her had done the same.

That led to her walking through the library, her fingers

trailing across the spines of the books she had previously discounted as mundane.

That day, insight rocked her world: all books were spells. Some were simple, some were more complicated, but every one aimed to change reality through the eyes and mind of a reader. The spell might be as simple as taking someone through a story puzzle to a story answer. Other books might make more extensive spells, whether fiction, history, or cookbook, each examining how the world was, and how it might yet be.

That was magic.

Then Sanne stumbled across the first of the truly hidden books, with lore and spells so deep they usually had nothing at all to do with the book's subject.

She began to take home stacks of books. Books on model airplanes, accounting, home repair, physics, and gardening. Books that Jerry would never suspect of having anything to do with witchcraft.

Her studies went deep. Her skills rose to a new level.

Sanne learned to look through the actual written words. She learned to hold a book in her hands and gain knowledge from the touch, or trace fingers across pages to learn from those who had come before her. Hidden in those books, for those who could read, was the teachings of centuries, the musings and makings of sages.

Sanne still read voraciously, and, from all appearances, eclectically. One never knew where the ancient lore would be tucked.

Across them all, even the mention of demon eggs was rare.

Sanne must get back to the land. Check that her spells

were holding. Make sure Johan was steady, or at least not rushing into a bad decision. She must find out more about Della Meyer and Terrance Hundley, without drawing their attention.

But first, she must figure out what to do with demon eggs.

As Sanne cut the box flaps, something fluttered to the ground.

It was a note from her sister, missed in the kids' unpacking.

Sanne, sorry to dump this on you, but again I thought it might be important. Found the box in a heavy metal thing, which I've disposed of. Wonder why it was stored that way. Mom, right? Love you, Marla.

A heavy metal box.

Sanne felt the blood drain from her face as her heart thumped.

A metal box, specifically designed to hold demon eggs inert.

Now, Sanne was sure: Angie's touch on the eggs and her own were irrelevant. The eggs had started incubating from the moment Marla had taken them from the metal box where her mother had kept them, to prevent this very thing.

Ah, crap.

Sanne texted her sister. Hey, sis. Maybe not send things through the mail—something valuable could get lost. Hang on to it all until we can talk? Love, Sanne.

With any luck, that would at least delay Marla's further cleanup efforts.

Demon eggs.

Sanne looked across the room at her many books, none of which had the answers she needed, and needed fast.

She would drive to the city with its huge public library, and trail fingers across the spines of as many books as she could, hoping against the odds that she would find one that knew more about demon eggs.

She needed new ancient lore.

CHAPTER

TWELVE

Della remembered the first time she'd been here at the MacKenzie land, when MacKenzie had given her and Terry a tour in his beat-up white pickup truck.

As they bounced along the rutted dirt road, Terry describing his history with various stumps and gullies, Della had been puzzled, then amused, to sense that someone had ensorcelled various locations on the land to make the place seem less interesting.

It was anything but. This land was rich with development possibilities, right off a highway, and close to town.

As she waited for Terry to return, she strolled around MacKenzie's house, assessing the area with a developer's eye, deciding how to connect an old farmer, reluctant to give up his land, and the developers ready to move.

Tomorrow, she'd meet with the other two developers on her list. They'd want answers and fast to decide if they wanted to dive into a bidding war. And that was where the big money was.

Della was in a fine mood. All the sticks she'd worked so

hard to arrange, so that they'd fall into place when she needed them, were poised and ready.

Today, though—today was a carrot day.

Terry pulled into the gravel drive. Johan MacKenzie stepped out of the passenger seat of the royal blue Mustang.

"Nice ride," MacKenzie said, in a tone of awe.

"Oh, hey. Check out the pony." Terry came around to MacKenzie's side and gestured. On the potholed driveway, a rippling light pattern emanated from under the passenger side door, forming a galloping mustang against the asphalt.

"Golly," MacKenzie said in genuine surprise.

This was one of Terry's skills, his way with clients. Male clients in particular. Terry had an easy manner, was affable and approachable. His delight in toys, machinery, and cars was contagious.

"You want to drive it?" Terry asked, with childlike glee, holding out keys.

"Oh, no, I couldn't."

"Sure you could."

"Haven't driven something like this in years. Wouldn't know how."

"Nothing to know. It's easy. Come on."

Terry was the perfect five-year-old boy: eager to share and taking genuine pleasure in seeing others enjoy his toys.

The two men went through another few rounds of ritual offer and refusal, which Della knew would shortly end with MacKenzie in the driver's seat. At last Terry pressed keys into MacKenzie's hands.

Della also knew that somewhere on this drive, Terry would work into the conversation that MacKenzie could have a car like this one, his very own, with all the extras he might like.

If the deal went through.

Della continued her stroll, eyeing the various fruit and fir trees that would need to be ripped out, the rise and fall of the land that would require bulldozing, and mentally prepared for the next day's negotiations.

Behind her, the Mustang roared to life, MacKenzie in the driver's seat. Della smiled.

Definitely a carrot day.

THIRTEEN

Sanne drove back from the city library in a dark mood.

The good news was that she had found five books of ancient magic lore, and had read them start to finish.

While the author-sages disagreed about the appearance of demon eggs, newly hatched demons, and demons in general, they were in surprising agreement about their behavior.

A demon baby, they wrote, was born hungry. It would eat almost anything, from trash to human flesh, but would have a particularly keen taste for priceless and irreplaceable objects of power. Like books of ancient lore.

The sage Harper speculated that this was why so few of the deeply magical books remained.

And so Sanne had not checked out the most precious of the books she'd found, but read and left them there. She could not risk them.

Then, after the demon baby's hunger was momentarily

eased, the young demon would want, most of all, to return home.

Home, it turned out, was in another dimension. To get there, the young creature would need to make a passageway, which required a particular sort of door. Those doors were energy-workers-- witches, sages, movers, and the rest. People like Sanne.

Unfortunately, those doors were often taken by surprise, and did not always survive the experience.

In some of the tomes, a list of names followed, names of sages who had sacrificed themselves, knowingly or unknowingly, to send a fast-maturing demon home, to prevent more dire destruction.

Attempting to destroy the eggs prior to hatching was most definitely not recommended. Some sages said it was impossible. Others said it could be done with extreme measures, but amounted to a clarion call to cross-dimensional creatures who might like a tasty snack. Or to the parents, who you definitely did not want visiting.

As Sanne pulled her car to the curb at her house, a pang of nostalgia went through her for the person she had been as she'd driven to the library, when she'd thought the eggs were a problem to be solved, rather than a pending disaster.

Worse than a just-hatched demon was a demon teenager. A demon, as it grew, became stronger. It gradually forgot about going home.

To say a mature demon could cause chaos and destruction was an understatement. The worst of history's earthquakes, floods, volcanic eruptions, tornadoes, and cyclones were just the beginning. Somehow, demons could cause planes to crash, famine to take hold, and epidemics to explode through landmasses.

Demons were bad news.

A hatchling was dangerous, but it was not exactly invincible. If you knew what you were doing, you had a chance.

And more importantly, the sages wrote, the demon egg could be contained. By metals, sand, dirt, and stone. Even hatchlings would not eat those things.

Now, Sanne understood her mother's metal box. Somehow her mother had come into possession of three demon eggs, and had done everything she could to keep them safely tucked away, unhatched, intact. She might have even intended to tell Sanne about them someday.

Then, when Jerry had died, Marla had decided to clean up.

Marla was always the neat one.

As for the hatching period, Sanne's guess was right: the moment the egg was taken out of its insulating container of metal, sand, dirt, or stone, it would begin to incubate. If one left such an egg in the open—or in a box of packing peanuts, which was the same to the egg—it would start the process of maturation.

Then it would hatch.

A hatchling demon moved terrifyingly fast. It would dart about, eating anything that held magic.

Which was everyone.

The best way to deal with demon spawn, the sages asserted and adamantly, was to make certain the egg never hatched.

Dirt. Sand. Metal. She had to halt the incubation.

Sanne replaced the cotton batting with sandy, gravelly fill taken from a nearby driveway. She wrapped the box in tin foil and tied it with garden wire, then put it in the trunk of her car, reasoning that the trunk was, after all, a metal box.

A good start. Maybe.

Dread crept through Sanne as she drove, imagining the eggs scratching in their shells, alive, eager to be free.

She blinked the vision clear, dismissed the tendrils of terror tugging at her mind. The last thing she needed was to work herself into a panic.

Next, the hardware store. She bought an old-fashioned metal tackle box and various spools of fencing wire, unsure what she would need.

She brought it all inside, setting things on the table next to the foil-covered box.

She sat in a chair and gazed at the box. To move the eggs from the silver-clad cardboard box to the better protection of the metal tackle box meant unwrapping them, and taking each one out.

Had the tinfoil been useless? Or was it all that had kept the demons from hatching? Her thoughts felt foggy.

Or maybe there were no demons, and the whole thing was her imagination.

She blinked, shook her head, confused. She stood and took a slow step away from the table, then another.

It had already begun.

Even here in her own domain, the cleared space of her home, she was affected by these creatures.

Sanne took a breath, let it out slow. She focused on her feet, and trickled an energetic line from the top of her head down through her spine, into the ground. Then beyond that, into the dirt below the house, the rock below that. The dark places beneath, far down, that humankind had yet not touched.

Her mind cleared somewhat.

She looked around the room for an appropriate tool.

There.

In each hand she took in a metal knitting needle. Stepping forward, she tapped the silver box that contained the eggs, and spoke a spell of gathering, of closing, of containment.

It must be a gentle spell, if the demons inside were ready to fight their way out. She wove a sleeping song, the tune soft in her throat.

Bit by bit she felt the tendrils of doubt and fog retract, the force within the eggs again become dormant.

Mostly.

The room at last felt silent, her mind clear.

The moment of peace was welcome. Then a chilling thought surfaced: in every book of lore that mentioned demon eggs, the sages had written in the singular.

One egg. Not a set of three.

Which meant that no magic worker had ever before been faced with three. Or, more likely, none who did so had survived to write about it.

Ah, crap.

Sanne's heart began to speed. She must separate them, and now. Bury them in the ground. She'd go out to Johan's land. The earth would hold them, if she put them deep enough.

She took the silver box under her arm and grabbed the tackle box by the handle. With her free hand, she took up car keys, and snatched her scarf from under the bed.

~

SANNE STOOD FROM DIGGING THE HOLE. THE scarf was thick around her neck from being looped many times to avoid it dragging in the dirt, or tangling around the shovel.

She eyed the foil-wrapped box sitting atop the loam of decades of fallen leaves.

The hole was two feet down, maybe a bit more, as deep as she could manage.

A hundred feet would be better.

Sanne crouched, then unwrapped the garden wire from the box, looping it around her wrist. Peeling back the tin foil, she revealed the old cardboard box. She ran her fingers over the flaps, wondering if there had once been a spell of sealing there.

Maybe the demon eggs had eaten that spell. She wouldn't put it past them.

She steadied her thoughts, muttered an enchantment of protection, and dug her hands into the gravel and dirt to find the first egg. As her fingers brushed it, she felt a faint sensation, as if something were reaching back.

As she paused, it faded.

Nerving herself, she slowly drew the green egg from the dirt and gravel.

In the light of this overcast spring day, the egg's surface had faded from the bright green of an unripe avocado to something a touch darker, blacker.

It was changing. Incubating.

As she set the egg on the blade of the supine shovel, her fingers came away sticky. Was the damned thing oozing? She wiped her hands on the dirt, thought she smelled a slight odd scent, something like burning rubber.

Gripping the shovel handle, she balanced the egg on the curved blade, slowly lowering it into the hole, egg between blade and dirt, until the shovel could go no deeper.

Tilting the handle upright to let the egg roll into the dirt, she pulled the shovel out of the hole.

The egg was stuck to the blade.

For a moment she stared, dumbfounded.

Impossible.

Demon eggs. It was not impossible.

She set the shovel down on the ground and unwrapped the wire on her wrist. As she spoke a spell of sundering, she passed the wire between the egg and the surface of the blade, as if flossing a tooth.

The egg rolled free onto the dirt.

Then it began to roll toward the box. Toward the other eggs.

"Oh, no, you don't," she hissed, grabbing the green thing between both hands.

Again, the sensation of being grabbed in return. Sanne straddled the hole. The first time, she had lowered it gently, concerned about cracking it open. At this point—no. Just get it in.

She aimed for the center of the hole, and dropped the egg.

Except that it stuck to her hands. She shook her hands, spoke a spell, spoke another, more urgently. The egg was attached to palms and fingers, as if with superglue.

Suddenly, the egg let go of one hand and began to roll up her arm, somehow grabbing her skin through two layers of fabric, defying gravity.

Sanne dashed to the box with the other two eggs. The egg stopped on her arm, and reversed itself, rolling down and into the space where it had been before, burrowing next to its siblings.

Sanne covered it with gravel and dirt, closed the box, rewrapped the foil, and tied it with the garden twine.

Breathing hard, she looked around at the hole, the shovel, the box.

Nowhere in the lore had there been any mention that unhatched eggs had independent volition.

Nowhere in the lore had they written of three eggs that clearly intended to stay together.

Her mind spun.

She could not, she decided, bury the three together. She was convinced that they must be separated to be quelled.

Somehow.

SANNE SET THE BOX IN HER TRUNK, CASTING another spell of somnolence.

Sleep, sleep, you little monsters.

She shut the trunk.

Johan's front door opened. He walked toward her. His posture spoke volumes.

"Johan, what's wrong?"

At first, he wouldn't meet her eyes. "Mama got worse. And my dad, he needs looking after. I promise you, the trees will be alright. I made sure of it."

Sanne's heart sank. "Johan, what happened?"

"I had to sign. Della and Terry promised to make sure, about the heritage trees."

Della and Terry.

Sanne had known those two would move fast, but this fast?

"Johan, no. That woman is—" What could she say? A witch? "Not to be trusted."

"Ah, they've been good to me, Susanne. Helping me out. They've made it easy."

"Yes, that's what they..." *what they do.* "Johan, what did you sign?"

His gaze traced the house, trees, fields. "It's in escrow." When at last his eyes met Sanne's, they were wet. "I did what I had to do, Susanne. For me and mine."

Me and mine.

Sanne felt the blow hit deep. She had hoped—foolishly, in retrospect—to bury the eggs, then visit the trees. Lean on them. Let the trees hold her small human concerns in their ancient wisdom.

Self-disgust flashed through her. She wanted to ask the trees to comfort her and give her advice, but what had she done for them lately? Found out Della Meyer and Terrance Hundley's names?

Johan's look was earnest. His eyes were almost begging.

She could see that he ached for her to say that she under-stood. That it was okay.

It wasn't okay. But Sanne knew he was struggling. How could she tell him that the land was more important than his family?

Instinct drove her to action. She unwrapped the scarf, held out the unreasonably long length of red, orange, and green to Johan.

"This is for you," she said.

"Oh, no. I don't need another scarf."

"I made it. I want you to have it."

"You made this?" he looked at it again, impressed. "That's sure special. But I couldn't take it from you." He patted his belly. "I put on weight last year. Good insulation. Don't really need it."

"A gift, Johan. It would mean so much to me, that you have it." Sanne's voice cracked.

That caught his attention.

"Sure, then." He took the length, awkwardly holding it high, folded it in half, and again, until it was in the shape of a fat pillow. He tucked it under his arm.

Not around his neck. Sanne's heart sank.

"You'll wear it?" she asked.

"Since you made it. Be my favorite. Not so cold today. We'll get a spring snap yet, see if we don't. Then, you bet."

Sanne had bet that the trees could wait. Then she had bet that she could handle the eggs.

Right now, she wasn't inclined to bet on much of anything.

CHAPTER

FOURTEEN

But what if she said no?

It was only a diamond.

Terry combed his thick hair back with his fingers, and grinned.

"Baby, there's no one like you. We're a great team. You know it. I know it. So here's what I'm thinking…"

His smile vanished.

"Bunch of bullshit," he snapped at the scowling image in the mirror. "Get one chance, you moron. You fuck it up, I never forgive you."

Della had called him lover, once. In the dark of the night, under the sheets, something lit up in her eyes, and the word was on her lips.

Lover.

He gave the mirror another wide smile. "Della, darling —" that was good. Kind of poetic, right? "Love of my life. Want to share it with you. Let's—"

Ah, God. She'd hate that kind of crap. His smile turned hard.

"You and me, babe. How about it?" he asked. "Take the damned ring. It's expensive."

He snarled at himself, turned his back on the mirror, glared at the rest of the bathroom. The Jacuzzi tub, fancy toilet, thick towels.

All the things that made life worth living, he thought sourly.

Okay, then: he'd say nothing. He'd put out his hand, give her that look she liked.

She'd probably be annoyed.

"What?" she'd ask.

He'd give her a great big smile, and like a showman, open his fingers. There, on his palm, would be the glittering ring.

"Marry me," he muttered.

What if she said no?

His hand went to his pocket. Not the one with the special little velvet box that held the brilliant thing he couldn't figure out what to do with, but the other one, with the cute little toy Tesla he'd found in just the right color of pink. Somehow it comforted him, rubbing its little wheels with his thumb.

"It's not that complicated," he said to himself. "You're just stupid."

Maybe it was too soon. Two and a half years. Should he wait?

He couldn't wait. He couldn't bear a third anniversary of that first night together, without knowing that she loved him enough to say yes.

He'd gone to a lot of trouble these last two years to hide

money. A little here, a little there. Let her think some of his toys were more expensive than they were.

Della watched their finances like a hawk. He let her, collecting a tidy sum right under her nose so that he could buy this damned ring to impress her.

It would impress her. It had to.

What if she said no?

He could not bear it.

He could not wait, either.

He nerved himself to look in the mirror again, then stared. What did she see when she looked at him?

A mate? A bed-warmer? A handy errand boy?

He had no clue.

DELLA DROPPED HER KEYS AND PURSE ON THE table in the entrance-way.

Terry was in the apartment. She could practically smell him.

"Break out a bottle of '02, Terry," she called out. "We're celebrating."

MacKenzie had needed a bit more charm, some additional promises, and a few affectionate hand touches by which Della arranged a multi-pronged connection to his emotions, body, and spirit, to be sure he stayed in line.

She'd managed the entire transaction on heavy paper rather than electronically, correctly guessing he'd be more impressed.

Then MacKenzie had sat there for a long moment, pen in hand, hovering over the stack of papers. Della spoke gently, as if to an unsettled horse, while she laid out more spells, blanketing the room in brightness, optimism, and happiness. A glorious future awaited.

He'd signed.

MacKenzie had seemed deflated as she left the house, like a flattening tire.

The house and land that would soon be hers.

He'd recover. He'd be happier for it, too. Della was doing him a favor—she had given him the great gift of freedom, even if he didn't quite know it yet.

Besides, his land was doing nothing useful. In a couple of years' time, if all went well, twenty families could have houses there.

Once she managed Developer A, B, or C into contract, she'd have a new pot of gold. Not only that, she would have arrived at a new level of the game.

She stopped to gaze at the framed photo of the Azimut yacht. She could nearly feel the sun, smell the ocean, taste the champagne.

Well, she could have one of those three things right now.

In the kitchen was Terry. He had that familiar distracted look about him, as if he'd just woken from a nap.

"Did you hear me?" Della asked. "We're celebrating. The MacKenzie place is in escrow."

"Oh, that's great, Dell. I... I..." He trailed off.

Della waited for him to finish, then gave up.

"Just get the bottle, okay?"

"Yep, yep."

She brought two glasses, and he brought the chilled bottle. They met at the coffee table, couch positioned to offer them an expansive view of Marigold and the hills beyond.

Terry worked the cork and poured. They each held a glass of gently fizzing amber.

Della had been planning this moment since they arrived in Marigold, since the moment she had eyed the newly zoned farmland and decided to acquire it for development. This toast had been on her mind these last few days.

To us and our future. To our first day on the yacht. Something like that.

Or: *To families with beautiful, big homes in the hills.*

Memory brought her a flash of a small, dirty apartment that smelled of rancid oils, and the sickly sweet stink of insecticide.

She pushed it away, lifted her glass.

"We've worked hard," she began, clinking her glass to his. "One more step toward our future. Here's to—"

"I have something for you," Terry said, interrupting.

"You what?"

Terry stood, fumbling in his pocket. He glanced at her, then away, visibly nervous.

"I've got a thing. For you."

She bit back angry words, checked the conjuring she'd woven around him to be sure it was still tight, secure. It was.

"Damn it, Terry. Can't this wait?"

"I don't think so."

With her free hand she made an impatient gesture for him to continue.

He stopped, as if frozen, mouth hanging open.

"Get on with it," she said tightly. "I want my drink." Della was now truly annoyed.

"This. I got this for you." He tossed something on the couch at her side.

A small toy. A Tesla. In magenta. Not quite the same shade as hers, but close.

She picked it up, examined it, then put her attention back on Terry.

Across his face was childlike hope.

She suppressed a sigh. "Very nice, Terry. Thank you."

Oh well. She'd known he was broken when she took him on.

She patted the couch at her side. "Sit down. Let's drink to our success, shall we?"

He nodded, but glumly. What had he expected of her in response to a toy, when she had the real thing, parked outside?

They sipped in silence, Della staring out at the hillside.

"It's good, isn't it?" he asked after a bit, as if he didn't quite trust his own taste.

He surely meant the champagne. She had no idea what else he could be talking about.

"It's good," Della affirmed. "Though maybe a bit flat."

"Oh."

Next time, Della thought, maybe she'd celebrate by herself.

CHAPTER

FIFTEEN

As Sanne drove home from Johan's farm, she took the wrong turn at an intersection she'd navigated hundreds of times, forcing her to backtrack.

At home, she pulled to the curb, then realized that her house was on the other side.

The eggs were fighting back. She needed to know more.

If only her mother had left more than two words. She knew what they were—she'd labeled it. Why had she not left more, some explanation of how she had come by them? Some clues about what to do with them?

Or maybe she had.

A sudden conviction came to Sanne that one of the books her mother had left, that Jerry had burned that horrible night, had contained something about the eggs. Maybe more.

Fury blazed within her. Jerry had died leaving a mess with tangles that he didn't even believe existed.

She found herself praying that somewhere, in an afterlife, Jerry was being well-educated.

Where was she? Far from the present moment. She was sitting in her car, tightly gripping the steering wheel.

This wasn't right. One's mood was critically important to dealing effectively with powerful enchantments. The kind those demon eggs were throwing at her right now.

She must calm her anger, and fast. Then she would drive back to the library and look for more books.

With the eggs in the back, grabbing her focus every moment?

No. She must leave them in the house.

Sanne got out of the car, took the foil-wrapped box from the trunk, and crossed the street to her house.

At the front door, she stopped, confused.

It was not her house.

Holy crap.

Her mind was not entirely her own. The eggs were getting stronger.

She took in a slow breath, let it go, fighting the urge to speed things up. *To go faster, move more slowly,* went the old adage.

Sanne wove a slow spell of clarity. It did almost nothing.

She whispered the oldest grounding litany she knew, calling in the four elements, and the directions of the compass, placing herself in the middle.

Better.

Now she could feel the eggs in her arms, even if the box felt unimaginably heavy.

She took a step north, letting herself feel the pull of the earth's magnetic field. Then she stepped south, east, and west, claiming her place as a creature of this world.

Which the demon eggs were most certainly not.

Sanne looked around the street, found her house, and walked toward it.

The kids sat on the stoop, waiting.

Alarm washed through her. This situation was nothing like safe, not for Sanne. Far, far less for these children.

What the holy earth were they doing here?

"WHAT ARE YOU DOING HERE?" SANNE ASKED.

The three thirteen-year-olds exchanged uncertain looks.

"It's lesson day, Sanne," said Keyton.

"It is?" Sanne asked.

"And you're late," muttered Rufus.

Angie gave Sanne a worried look. "Are you okay?"

Sanne had never missed a lesson. She was never late. She might be sloppy about everything else, but not this.

Their faces were a mirror of her own deeply unsettled insides.

"What's in the box?" asked Rufus.

"Oh! Is it the eggs?" Angie asked excitedly.

This was not a conversation they could have.

Sanne wrapped her arms tightly around the box, muttering a spell of closure, of hiding, and then making a bubble around herself and the box, a boundary between the eggs and the kids. It took nearly all her focus.

"No class today," she managed.

This gained her expectant looks.

"What are we doing, then?" Angie asked, misunderstanding.

"Why's the box covered in tinfoil?" asked Keyton. "Is it to keep aliens from reading the egg's minds?"

Keyton's mock seriousness made the other two kids laugh. The sound vanished quickly in Sanne's sober expression. It was too close to the truth.

"Listen, guys," Sanne said, struggling for calm. "It's best that you go. Study whatever I gave you last week, and I'll see you next week. Okay?"

"What's wrong?" Rufus asked.

"Is it witch stuff?" Angie asked.

"You have a magic problem?" asked Keyton. "Oh, cool. We can help."

Sanne could sense the eggs scratching through the box, like tingles of electricity tugging against her skin.

"I mean it," Sanne said quietly.

With obvious reluctance the kids stood, slung bags over their shoulders, and thudded down the stairs to the street. They walked away, shoulders drooped, faces fallen.

As long as they were unhappy somewhere else, where they were safe.

Rufus was walking backward, watching Sanne.

"She's got that look," he said, "the one Angie gets when she's stuck on a problem."

The kids all stopped and turned to study Sanne.

"Like when I've got a bug in my code," Keyton said.

"You always tell us," Angie said to Sanne, "that if we get stuck on a problem, we should ask each other for help."

"Get another perspective," Rufus added.

"We have three of them," Keyton said.

"Can we help?" Angie asked.

As one, the kids took a slow step toward Sanne.

Damn, but this was her own fault. Sanne had taught them to think for themselves, to be stubborn in the face of adversity, and tenacious about finding solutions.

She had never taught them to care. She hadn't needed to.

"No," Sanne said, but softly, too softly, so they kept walking forward.

When they were close enough to hear her whisper, she did. "Listen to me," Sanne breathed. "This is serious stuff. Very dangerous. You're kids. Please go."

Sanne thickened her bubble, hardening it.

"In the last town where my family lived," Angie whispered back, "I was chased home from school. They called me names." The girl's usual happy look went hard, angry. "They threw rocks, Sanne. Some of them hit me. I threw them back. I know what danger looks like."

"Oh, Angie," Sanne said, moved.

Rufus swallowed, gave a sharp nod. "So, me, then. When I was five, my parents took in a stranger. Christian charity and all. One night, he snuck into my and my sister's room. We told my parents, and he's gone now, but we didn't tell them everything. I won't ever forget that night."

"Rufus," Sanne said, her voice full of emotion.

Keyton scowled, voice hard. "A gang of boys cornered me in an alleyway. Said they'd teach me to be a girl. I'm not telling you more than that, but I can show you my scar."

"Oh, cool. I have one, too," Rufus said to Keyton. "Right here on my forehead. From a baseball."

"Sanne, look," Keyton said. "Just like we don't really know you, you don't really know us. We know how bad things can get. We know what danger is."

Angie nodded. "And we know who friends are. If you need us, we're here."

Sanne was trembling with the effort of keeping the eggs contained, not to mention her eyes from tearing up.

She shook her head. "This would have to be a secret. A real one. I can't ask you to keep things from your parents."

Rufus snorted. Keyton smirked.

Angie sighed. "You think we tell them everything now?"

"Then you don't remember being thirteen," Rufus added.

"Truth," Keyton said with feeling.

"Sanne," Angie said. "You don't have to tell us anything you don't want to. We could just keep you company for a bit, so you know you're not alone. Hang out. We could knit for a while."

"Yeah," Rufus agreed. "We could knit."

We could knit.

All at once, Sanne had an idea.

SANNE CLOSED THE DOOR, KIDS AND EGGS INSIDE. She felt the gravity of the actions she was taking.

She met the gazes of each of her charges, reflecting that she'd agreed to teach them programming and computer science. Maybe some wildcrafting. The occasional knitting.

Not witchcraft. They had no idea what they were stepping into.

Neither did Sanne, for that matter.

They had just told her that they knew what danger was, and they had come in willingly.

As for magic... she recalled their reaction to the scarf. They knew it when they saw it.

She searched their faces, looking for consent of mind, heart, and spirit. Finding it, she nodded, and set the box of eggs on the table.

But how much to involve them? She could work silently and keep the kids as blind participants. The less they knew, the easier it would be for them to forget.

The world of spirit and magic was like that—if you didn't know what to look for, if you didn't have repeated exposure to this way of seeing, of being, it was easy to lose the memory and explain it away. A trick of the light, or of the mind. Something that hadn't really happened.

And the less they knew, the less they could say later to their friends and parents about Sanne the witch.

With the greater part of her focus on the box at the center of the room, holding it in as much somnolence as she could, Sanne gestured Rufus to the south end of the space, Angie to the east, Keyton to the west.

She walked the room in a circle, picking up what she needed as she went.

The eggs were dozing, but she could feel them struggling to wake, wanting to move, act, be free.

By contrast, the three kids seemed alert, watching her. How much could she rely on them? She reviewed what they had told her outside.

They had trusted her with their secrets. They were willing.

"Rufus," she said, to the suddenly wide-eyed boy, as her

slow pace took her closest to him. "Can you remember a time when you weren't sure if something would work out? Maybe you were afraid. Then it did work out, and you felt stronger for it?"

He nodded.

"Good," Sanne said. "Hold that feeling, that strength. Let it be like a fire inside, keeping you safe."

As she cleared the space around him, she felt him kindle something within, something young, vibrant, and alive.

Still slowly circling the room, she came to the east.

"Angie, do you recall a moment when you weren't sure what was going on, but you trusted yourself anyway? It worked out, and later you felt larger than you had been before?"

Angie nodded soberly.

Sanne smiled. "Can you keep that feeling of knowing, of seeing, of being big?"

"Yes," Angie said quietly.

Sanne cleared the area around Angie, felt the girl holding the space where she stood, like a circling hawk.

"Keyton," Sanne said as she came close. "Do you remember when you first moved between aspects of yourself, and knew that was your truth? That no one and nothing could hold you in one place, frozen? Can you feel that freedom now?"

Keyton gave a sharp nod. A swirl began around Keyton, like a small vortex, like the flow of a river. Sanne cleared space around zir.

While keeping her attention pinned to the box at the center of the constellation, she sensed into each of the three directions, to see if the kids were holding them.

They were.

Sanne permitted herself the briefest flash of pride as she continued her slow circuit, handing each of the three a metal crochet needle. She came to a stop at the north part of the room.

"To weave something new," Sanne said, "there must be someone to weave. We four are that someone." Sanne held up her own needle. "There must be a strand to work with. Yarn, thread, cord. Anything, really. Imagine that a line is coming to you from the person on either side, and that you are sending your own to them. Imagine this as clearly as you can. And then, take the line, and begin."

Sanne sent out etheric lines, and took the ones that came back to her. The four of them began to move their needles in the air, grabbing the lines with their free hand, looping and chaining stitches together.

It was working. With the vision she had cultivated across a lifetime, Sanne saw the fabric they were weaving build in intensity and brilliance.

Sanne was impressed at how fully the kids had taken on the work. "Beautiful," she said. "Now, we change the stitch. Instead of sending to either side, send a strand up and over the table, and another, under, to the person across from you."

They did. After some minutes, Sanne spoke again. "We've made a flattened sphere around the table. Can you see it, almost? Maybe feel it?"

Eyes wide, they nodded.

"Keep your lines strong," she said.

The envelope they had woven around the table and around the box of eggs was sparkling and lucid.

This was step one.

Sanne took a breath. Things were about to get tricky.

And yes, Sanne decided, she was going to need to tell them what was going on.

As Sanne kept one eye on the box of eggs, she gave the kids a much-abridged version of how they had come to this moment.

"Demon eggs?" Rufus asked.

"They looked like emu eggs," Angie said.

"Yes, that's what they do," Sanne replied. "They mimic. They hide."

"How did you get them?" Keyton asked.

With this talk, which brought thinking and reasoning, their attention was fading, and the weave around the table was weakening. Sanne motioned in the air with her needle, strengthening the structure.

"I inherited them," Sanne answered, picking up spools of fencing wire from the counter. She walked the circle, handing them out.

She would not, she decided, tell that she had never done anything like this before, that she wasn't at all sure it would work. But she would tell them that it was dangerous.

"This could go bad," Sanne said. "You've done great work. I can take it from here. Now's a good time for you to go."

Angie was already shaking her head.

"This is dangerous," Sanne added. "I know you want to

help, but this is about to be some serious sh—" She blinked. "Shtuff."

Angie suppressed a smile.

"We don't want to leave, Sanne," Rufus said quietly. She saw his belly-spirit burn hot, and knew that he meant it. The two others nodded in agreement.

They had been right: they hadn't known each other that well. She knew them a lot better now. She saw their courage, loyalty, and insight.

She would not, she decided, tell them that they might well be defending the town of Marigold. That would be too much pressure.

But she would let them do it.

"All right," she replied. "Next, we separate them."

She approached the center—the table, the box, the eggs.

"Advice, in case this goes badly wrong." Sanne put her fingertips lightly on the tinfoil wrapping, grounding like mad into the bedrock deep below the floor. "A demon's power is all about your own darkness. It draws from you what you fear, what you loathe in yourself. Think of it as a very nasty mirror, showing some maybe true things, but making them larger. They'll seem real. So if you notice things going strange." She untwisted the garden twine ribboning the tinfoil. "Don't believe everything you think."

An amused exhale from Rufus.

"Remember when we learned to crochet hats in the round?" Sanne asked.

"Mine was so tiny it didn't fit my head," muttered Rufus.

"That's what we want. Start with the wire. Make a basket, about the size of an emu egg." She gave them a moment to think that through. They began to work their wire, crocheting rounds, building them into baskets.

Who to start with? Which of them might be best at recognizing their own darkness?

She motioned to Keyton to join her at the table, to set zir wire basket on the surface.

The sound deep in her throat became a lullaby, one her mother had taught her long ago. She imbued it with the quality of dirt, sand, and stone, what the eggs were still packed in, as she unwrapped the tinfoil and opened the flaps of the box.

The song became a chant, an invitation, a spell, one that slowed to a cadence that took the room into a deep, thick place, as if they were in an underground cavern. Sanne drew from the elements of the circle: fire, air, water. Earth. Mostly earth.

Things of this world. Not of the demons' world.

She brushed away dirt and pebbles to reveal a bit of green shell.

The eggs were sleeping. She could feel it. The spell was holding.

Brushing back more of the pebbled dirt, Sanne wrapped fingers around the egg. She lifted it out, holding the green-black thing in her hand. It was not sticky. She carefully placed it wide-side down into Keyton's wire pouch.

It did not grip her skin. Still asleep.

She held the spool as Keyton continued to crochet the wire around the egg, tighter until it closed atop the green shell.

Keyton made a tie-off with the wire. Sanne used cutters to free the end.

The wrapped egg was secure.

As one, the four of them let out a breath.

Two more to go.

RUFUS WAS BOUNCING EAGERLY, SO SANNE brought him forward next.

Into his wire basket Sanne set the second egg, holding it steady while he finished his egg-shaped pouch. At the top of the green egg, Rufus fastened the weave and knotted it in place. Sanne snipped off the end.

Two demon eggs, caged in metal. Separated from each other. Which would weaken them.

Sanne hoped.

Angie had the benefit of being last, so her work was further along. Sanne took the last egg from the box and set it in the wire basket.

She felt something trying to come awake.

As Angie weaved quickly around the egg, Sanne's phone rang. She felt the structure of the sphere weaken from the sound. The depth of the room began to flatten.

"Ignore that," she said, mostly herself. "Stay focused."

One of the parents wondering where their kids were? Had they gone over lesson time?

What if the parents were outside right now, about to break in, to find their children? What would they think of this?

What had Sanne been thinking, involving the kids?

The ring continued, annoyingly, and at last ended.

Only an inch of the green-black shell remained to cover.

"Give it to me," Sanne said. Angie handled her the needle. Sanne began to mutter an old spell, then realized it was the wrong one. She went silent as she rushed to finish the weave.

"Sanne," Angie said.

"Not now," Sanne said, looping and hooking, looping and hooking.

"Sanne, the egg."

"What about it?" Sanne asked, feeling her focus fraying.

"There's a crack."

A crack in the egg?

Her phone rang again.

A crack in the egg.

Sanne looked around the room, saw the sphere around her was gone, the kids were scared, and that she had lost her grounding entirely.

The demon was starting to break free.

"Come on, guys," Keyton said "Go back to your places. Pick up your needles. We have to make a sphere again, while Sanne fixes this."

Sanne blinked, trying to understand. She saw the kids moving, heard the words, but everything was muddy, as if it were all coming through water.

In her hands, something was stirring. She looked down to where the green-black egg was tucked inside a nearly complete pouch of gray wire. A mere half inch remained uncovered.

What was wrong with her, that she had put her needle aside? She took it up again, paused.

Her phone was ringing.

No, it wasn't.

A sob caught in her throat. The needle was too heavy. She wasn't sure how to finish. Whose fingers were these?

She would be called a witch. No one would hire her for anything. She'd starve.

"Sanne," Angie said. "Don't believe everything you think."

"Don't," Sanne said, gripping the needle and hooking the wire. "Believe." She made a loop, pulled through. Another loop, another stitch. "Everything." Her thoughts were clearing a bit as the kids brought the sphere back to vibrancy. "You," she said. Another stitch.

"Think," they all said together, with feeling.

The final stitch and she closed the pouch. Sanne felt the creature struggle inside. She tied off and knotted, clipping the spool free.

The cracked shell had brought with it a stench. Across the room was a stink. The scent of rotting fish, but also nothing like it. It smelled like dread.

But Sanne could focus again.

She looked at the kids. They looked back, uncertain.

"Is it okay now?" asked Angie.

"I think so. Thanks to you three."

"We couldn't have done it without you," Keyton replied.

"Didn't bring our crochet needles," Rufus said.

"Or eggs," Angie added.

Weak smiles all around.

Sanne laid a layer of tinfoil in the metal tackle box, then another. One by one, she gingerly moved the eggs into the tackle box, packing it with dirt and foil.

The kids moved in close, handing her wads of silver. In moments, the box was closed, latched.

The room felt clearer.

"I need to get these into the ground. That last one, especially. And fast."

"We'll come with you," Rufus said.

Sanne shook her head. "Your parents will be expecting you home. Or picking you up soon."

"Oh, right," Rufus replied.

Had Sanne's phone really rang? She went to it. It had. There was a message from Johan.

Susanne, it read. I might need a lawyer pretty quick. Know anyone?

The difficult magic they had just completed had left Sanne feeling deeply drained. Johan would need to wait.

She turned to the kids.

"You three...." The kids looked up from their texting. "I don't know how to thank you."

"I do," Angie answered. "Let us come with you and help finish this."

"But your parents—"

"—have agreed that since you're going wildcrafting this afternoon, we should go with you," Keyton said.

"Maybe we'll learn something," Angie said.

"My dad said to tell him if we find a good patch of morels," Rufus said.

"We told them it could take all afternoon," Keyton added.

"Did you?" asked Sanne with humor. "Who's in charge here, anyway?"

"The eggs?" suggested Angie.

The eggs.

Sanne let out a long exhale.

"All right. But first..." She went to a cupboard, brought out a bar of dark chocolate, broke off a piece for herself, and put the rest on the counter. "Ancient Mayan warriors knew that chocolate was a source of strength and courage."

It was good chocolate.

Sanne went to the bookshelf and took the crystal her mother had given her when she was a child. She tucked it into her pack.

"Time to go," she said.

CHAPTER

SIXTEEN

Della adjusted her sunglasses. The spring sun had finally topped the mountains and found the town sidewalk.

She held a latte in hand as she strode back from the cafe. There was still a nip of cold in the air.

Her phone buzzed. It was Terry. She frowned. He usually texted.

"What?" she asked.

"Babe, I'm just the messenger," he said. "It's MacKenzie. Tried to talk him down, but he's not listening."

"Already signed. Doesn't matter."

"He's saying he's still got the five-day review."

"Too late by a day. Nice try, though," Della replied.

"That's what I thought, too. He says, Monday was a state holiday. Something about birds. Says it counts."

Della knew real estate law forward and back—she had to, to be the kind of broker she was. She knew all the ways a deal could slip through the cracks.

But each state had its own twists and turns. And holidays.

"Has an attorney contacted you?" she asked.

"Nope."

"Me neither. Good. We can fix this. Someone talked to him, since he signed. Do you know who?"

"No idea."

"I'm headed back," Della said, walking faster. "Pick me up out front in five. We'll go have a talk with Mr. MacKenzie. Get his head screwed back on straight."

"You got it, babe."

Della would find out who had changed his mind and get them out of the way. Hard.

"You've had coffee?" she asked.

"A bit."

She took another deep swallow. "I'll save you last the sip of mine."

"You're the best, Della."

"Five minutes."

SEVENTEEN

Sanne drove the four of them to the land.

She sensed the creatures in the trunk, though they were in a metal box and pouches of wire. Caged and contained, yet she knew they were there, felt them struggle to wake.

At Johan's house, Sanne grabbed the tackle box from the trunk, slung her pack over a shoulder, and led the three kids into the barn to get a shovel.

"Wouldn't this be better?" asked Angie.

"What is it?" Rufus asked.

"Post-hole digger," Angie answered, hoisting the narrow double-shovel. "Makes holes deeper, more easily. Just about the right size for eggs."

"Gold star, Angie," Sanne muttered.

Shovel and post-hold digger in hand, Sanne took them into the trees, but far from the grove.

As they went, Sanne paused to pick bright green shoots from the ground.

"Isn't that stinging nettle?" asked Angie.

"Sure is."

"Ow."

"Not if you know how," Sanne said, tucking the thorned stems into her shirt pocket. "I'll teach you sometime."

An optimistic statement, she thought grimly. But there was no point in telling them just how dangerous this was.

At a fallen log, Sanne broke off the white and orange frill of Turkey Tail. A twig of cedar slid into a pocket. A hand-sized stone went into her pack.

As they walked, Sanne felt keenly the grove of ancient trees, distant.

She would go nowhere near them with the eggs.

They walked under cloud and tree shadow, and stopped at a ring of alders, in the shade of tall fir. There they dug a deep hole while flickers called and squirrels chittered.

Angie had been right: the post-hole digger worked far better than the shovel. Between the four of them the digging went fast, but it was Rufus who ended up with the tool, burrowing with glee.

As Rufus dug to the limit of the hole digger, Sanne softly spoke spells of protection, calling in the power of earth.

She clicked open the metal tackle box and took out the first egg, wrapped in its wire pouch. She dropped a piece of Turkey Tail into the hole, then the wire-wrapped egg. It slid down into the dark earth.

Rolling nettle between her fingertips, which stung, she dropped that on top.

A powerful fungus, and plant, to hold the egg secure in the earth.

They filled the hole with earth. When it was nearly filled

in, Sanne set the stone she had taken into the soil. The four of them covered it flat with dirt and leaves. Sanne spoke a spell of closure and sealing.

Solid earth to hold the sleeping creature safe from the world.

One down.

THEY CROSSED A SMALL STREAM TO GET TO THE other side of the property, the second point of the equilateral triangle Sanne had in mind. There, Sanne gathered two more hand-sized rocks.

They came to a towering, tangled hill of blackberry, with canes an inch thick. The four of them crowded together and in a small opening, dug another hole. Sanne spoke spells, dropped in the fungus. In went the second egg, followed by the nettle.

She capped the hole with the second stone and covered it with dirt. She stood atop the recessed stone where the egg was buried. Through her feet, she felt into the ground, down and down.

No sense of the demon egg. The earth held it securely.

"Onward," she said softly.

The third spot was in an open field, close to Johan's house, though with the rise and fall of the land, the house was hidden.

The ground was harder here, with thick grass a barrier. It took a bit longer, but between shovel and post hole digger, the four made a deep third hole. Sanne muttered spells.

She had kept this one for last, thinking that it would be weaker without its fellows. As she took the cracked egg from the tackle box, she felt a twist in her gut, a darkening of the already overcast day, a sharp pang of doubt, and a flickering of fire in memory.

"Get back," she breathed to the kids. They took a few steps away.

She turned the egg in her hands, whispering a spell of separation, of things going to correct places.

It shuddered under her touch. The shell was sticky.

Trembling, Sanne knelt, set the egg on the dirt at the edge of the hole. It let go of her skin. The pouch—the metal cage around it—held.

Now, all it needed to do was to obey the laws of gravity.

She touched a fingertip to the wire-weave around the egg and nudged it forward into the hole. It resisted a bit, but gave in to her push.

Then it hung over the opening, suspended.

"Crap," Sanne mouthed.

Next, the egg then reversed course from the hole. It came toward Sanne, following her retreating finger. It left the ground like a plane, coming faster and faster at her head.

The kids made sounds. Words. Shock.

Sanne acted without thought, bringing the heel of her hand forward, an instinct from who-knew-where, as the wire-wrapped egg flew at her face.

The egg crunched under the force of the blow, fell to the ground. Bits of wetness splattered in all directions, and floated hovering in the air like bright fog. Around the egg, the dirt was flecked as if with tiny patches of glittering ice.

A sound emerged, unlike anything she had ever heard.

A moan. A train horn. A cougar's distant scream. A too-close gasp.

She knew, now, what a hatching demon sounded like.

The kids backed away even further, without Sanne telling them to.

Sanne had known this might happen. From her studies, she was aware of the risk. She knew what she must do if it hatched, if she couldn't bury it.

And that it might kill her.

First, get the hatchling's attention. Fully. Keep the kids safe.

Sanne leaned forward to where the crushed thing lay at the edge of the hole.

It had cracked like safety glass, retaining the general shape, though wire and egg were flattened from the blow. Jagged lines ran through the green-black shell. The surface gleamed with wetness.

With her non-sticky hand, Sanne felt into her pack and pulled out her mother's crystal. She reached out toward it, the crystal on her palm.

"Hello," she said as the demon emerged from shell and wire. "Come to me."

The demon hissed out of the cracks, like sparkling steam, in streams of iridescence, a brilliant smoke that curled toward Sanne.

Sanne must become a door to another world.

SANNE GROUNDED DEEP AND FAST INTO THE DIRT and bedrock below. She connected to air, the water of the land's aquifer, and to any fire in a half-mile radius—any neighbor houses with furnaces, water heaters, and stoves.

She tuned her mother's crystal, making it into a bright beacon. An offering.

Then she dropped every one of her own defenses.

The creature swirled in the air, like spiraling trails of glitter. She could almost feel it looking around at this strange land, trying to orient itself.

"This way," she said. "Come."

The demon floated toward Sanne.

According to the books, this would be a hard moment. She might survive, she might not. At best, it would leave her spirit, body, and mind injured, or broken.

There was no better way. Get the demon home, leave their world that much less troubled.

Protect the kids.

The demon hatchling leaned toward her—she wasn't sure how she knew, but she did—then began to fall toward her, like a toddler in a stumbling, falling run toward a parent.

As it came, Sanne fought to keep herself open, to think like the door this creature would need open to create its passageway home.

Would it come through the crystal? Or through her hand, sticky with its essence?

There were only a few feet between the demon and Sanne, yet she felt the otherworldly approach as if from far away. Its speed increased as if a huge bird flew at her face.

Dimly, she heard the kids shout.

The structure of Sanne's being seemed to stretch and

creak. She would never have guessed that she could flex in those particular directions, and yet she must.

The creature crashed through her, skittering from edge to edge, leaving footsteps and smudges on the walls and floors of her consciousness.

Then it was gone.

She blinked awake, alert, back into the physical world. Overhead, clouds were thinning, the sun laying a gentle warmth across her face.

Sanne looked around, bewildered. Had it passed through her and gone home? Was that it?

Keyton was pointing, his expression stark. "It went that way."

"You sure?" Sanne croaked.

"Oh, yeah," Keyton replied with feeling, swallowing.

"That was…" Rufus began, shook his head, lacking the right word. "But where did it go?"

Angie, who looked more than a little nauseated, said: "To look for the other eggs?"

To look for the other eggs.

"Crap," Sanne said adamantly.

Angie was right: the demon hatchling knew it had siblings. It didn't want to go home without them.

Sanne groaned. She attempted to stand, her limbs not entirely cooperating. The kids helped her. She took a wide-legged stance, as if she were on rough seas.

"That was not what you were expecting, was it," said Keyton, watching Sanne's face.

"Not quite," Sanne replied.

The only thing worse than having a just-hatched

demon use you as a door to get home was not having it use you at all.

"If it's gone back to find the other eggs, let's go get it!" Rufus said excitedly.

"Sure, let's split up," Sanne muttered, "and go search for the monster."

As the kids looked ready to do just that, she quickly added, "No, no, no. That was a joke. A poor one. We stay together."

"What now?"

What now, indeed?

Sanne took a shaky breath. She was struggling just to stand. She felt as if a bull had come through her mind and broken all the doors and windows.

She looked around, wondering what it would see, this demon hatchling. An odd place, this world, the only thing familiar the memory of its siblings who it could no longer feel.

It would go looking for them. It would search and search but not find the other two eggs that were buried deep, and sealed under spells of hiding, and stone.

After the demon baby was unable to find its siblings, it would look for the next most familiar thing it knew: Sanne.

Then it would tear its way home. With frightening clarity, Sanne realized that the demon had not even tried to make a passageway home. It had only walked by. She shuddered.

When it gave up looking for its siblings, it would want to eat, with a keen preference for anything that held power.

Sanne was both meal and door.

Her mind flashed to another great power, here on the land: the trees.

"It'll be back," she said. "In the meantime…"

What?

She scratched the back of her head, which had begun to itch from deep inside. Her body and spirit were rattled, torn. She needed to realign herself. She needed powerful medicine.

"This way," she said.

EIGHTEEN

Terry revved his royal blue Mustang just as Della got in.

"Really?"

He grinned. Della rolled her eyes. "Just get there without being pulled over, Terry."

"You got it, babe."

As he drove, she watched Marigold go by. Little houses, small churches. A thrift store, an old movie theater. Quaint.

Or run down. Depending on what you were selling, and to whom.

Della had never lived in a place like this before. She wasn't sure she liked it. Everything took longer because people needed to think it through, talk it out with everyone they knew, bring it to some group or another.

Gossip wasn't so much a way of passing along news as it was the town thinking out loud.

But there was opportunity here. Land to develop. Commerce to be had. Money for Della, if she played her hand right.

It all started with MacKenzie's land sale.

Off by one day. One damned day. If she had gotten him to sign one day sooner...

If this deal fell through, this close to the jackpot, her credibility would be badly dented. She'd be known as the broker who couldn't make it happen. Word would get around, and developers would wonder if she were reliable.

No. This would close. She would fix it.

They came to a stop sign. Della scowled at a yard, unmowed, thick with grass and the chaos of spring weeds. They left the town, headed into the hills.

They passed farmland, broken fences, overgrown fields, sagging barns. So much in disrepair. Unused.

Wasted. Which was why the county had re-zoned to allow this sort of suburban growth.

The area needed infrastructure. Water, sewer, turn-lanes, sidewalks. Have people live on this land, instead of holding out hope for a past that would never come again.

Gravel crunched under the tires as Terry pulled into MacKenzie's driveway. As they got out of the car, Johan stepped out of his front door to meet them.

Della put on her warmest smile and strode to meet him, feeling into the etheric connections she'd built with him across multiple meetings, to be sure he stayed coop-erative.

She couldn't feel him.

"Morning, Johan," she said, reaching out a hand to him. He stared at the hand, looking uncertain, and didn't offer his own in return. She withdrew hers, struggling to keep her smile. "How are you this morning?"

"Della. Terry. I just..." He took a breath. "Just want an

attorney to look over the contract. You don't mind, do you?"

Something had changed in MacKenzie. He had a completely different tone and look, and Della couldn't get in. What had happened?

"Of course not," Della said warmly, cuing Terry's look of agreement with her own. "What a lovely scarf." She could feel the damned thing. It was more than it seemed. "May I touch it?"

"I suppose," he said slowly.

He didn't know what it was, exactly. Not consciously. But he felt it.

Della stepped forward. Johan stepped back.

"Looks handmade," Della said with an admiration that was only partly feigned. "Who made this beautiful thing?" Her voice was a spell of reassurance, swirling around the two of them like a snowglobe of peace and security.

For a moment, it seemed to work. "My friend Susanne," he answered. "A bit nippy this morning."

"It sure is." It wasn't now, though. "Looks so soft," Della said, wrapping the air around MacKenzie in bright, sweet swaddling. "May I feel the fabric, Johan. Hmm? Yes?" *So safe,* her words said. *I'm your friend.*

With all the magic Della had wrapped around him, the man should be brain-fogged and compliant. Yet he took another slow step back, his face a map of conflict.

"Susanne, you say," Della purred, following close. She reached MacKenzie, who could not seem to back up as fast she approached. She brushed the fabric with her fingertips.

A masterful spell. Well-woven by someone who knew what they were doing.

This must be the same someone who had, for some mysterious reason, slowed time in downtown Marigold.

Perhaps the same someone who was confusing MacKenzie now, and threatening Della's business.

Della was no longer amused. The kitten had claws, all right. It was an alleyway tomcat who, left unchecked, would cost her this deal.

MacKenzie tugged free the tail in Della's hand, and stepped aside.

"Could I try it on?" Della asked, pumping seductive power into her words. "I'm so cold," she said daintily, giving him the look of a small, adorable creature.

His expression flickered and his resistance broke. He reached across himself with both arms for the scarf, to take it off and hand it to Della.

As he did, Della saw the scarf's magical flow shift to pass through his arms, to cross his heart, and spike up and down his spine.

MacKenzie's posture shifted abruptly. He stepped away decisively.

Damn.

Della was done being nice.

"Where would I find this Susanne," she asked, her voice flat, "this good friend of yours, Johan?"

For a moment his gaze went distant, then came back to her.

He lifted a hand and pointed. "There."

~

Coming toward them from the nearby fields was a woman and three teenagers.

The woman was a mess. Slumped, mouth slack, gaze refocused as she stumbled forward. Her hair was in disarray, her pants covered in dirt.

This was the magic worker who had woven a scarf that now jeopardized Della's deal? This was the one who had slowed time in downtown Marigold? This?

As the woman approached, Della looked her over with second sight, and took a good etheric sniff to see what she was about.

A tangle of energies, the woman was, her defenses confused, haphazard. As messy as her hair.

The problem might be simpler than she'd thought. This kitten would be easy to put down.

Della began a simple spell to intensify what was already there: confusion, sluggishness, a fractured self.

"Hello," the woman said to Della. She looked dimly surprised, as if only just now noticing the two visitors.

"You must be Susanne," Della said pleasantly, as she fed more power into the cracks in the other woman's edges. "Are you all right?"

"No," Susanne said simply.

"Anything we can do to help?" Della asked with concern, reaching out to take the other woman's hand, who, to her surprise, let her.

The hand was cold and sticky. Della tried to build a line into her, but it got tangled and bent in on itself, as if becoming just as confused as the woman's etheric field.

Susanne made a small grunt and took her hand back. Her heavily lidded gaze went to MacKenzie. "Meant to give you this earlier, Johan, but things…" She took a breath. "Happened." She dug into her pocket and brought out a phone, thumbed it, put it to her ear. "Marla. You practice in my state, right? Do me a favor, talk to a friend? Thanks."

Susanne held out the phone to MacKenzie.

Practice.

There was a lawyer on the other end of that call. The moment a formal conversation happened, the deal was in trouble. The money was fine, but some of the other things Della had promised to MacKenzie were more than a little vague. A good lawyer would find them.

Della had to stop MacKenzie from taking the call. She turned all her attention on him.

"Johan, listen to me," Della said urgently. "No one will offer you more money than I have. You've got bills coming due, and problems mounting. This deal will fix it all. Your debt, gone."

"I know, I know—I just—"

"Your parents. Remember," she said, "Terry and I are seeing to your parents. At our own expense, Johan." Small money compared to big, but MacKenzie had been impressed when Della had showed him the invoices. "We want your mom and dad taken care of, too. Don't you?"

"Yes," MacKenzie said, color and alarm coming to his face. "Of course I do."

"Of course you do," Della echoed passionately, struggling to get through the scarf to MacKenzie.

"Johan," Susanne said softly, "you got coffee inside?

"Sure thing, Susanne."

To Della's dismay, he took the offered phone from Susanne.

"Thanks." Susanne shuffled to the door, Della's spells clinging to her like fog, but not seeming to affect her. Was she already too broken?

As Della fought the scarf to try to keep MacKenzie's attention from the phone, Susanne went into the house, trailed by the three teens.

MacKenzie's hand, the one holding the phone, began to tremble under the force of Della's attack. He wrapped both hands in the tails of the scarf, and gave Della an apologetic smile. "I'm going to need to take this."

He turned to follow Susanne inside, leaving Della and Terry outside alone.

"Babe?" Terry asked softly, after the door was shut. "What just happened?"

Della was working to keep her rising fury contained. She spun it tight inside herself, a hot core within. A line. A spear. A weapon.

After a moment, Terry spoke again. "What do we do now?"

MacKenzie had been persuaded before. He would be persuaded again. All that stood in the way was Susanne and her damned scarf.

Della would find a way.

"You stay here," Della said, as she walked forward.

CHAPTER
NINETEEN

Inside Johan's house, Sanne struggled to think. The stomp of a demon hatchling through her had messed her up, and no question about it. She felt as if she were striding through muddy water, struggling to see, her judgment and focus not even sending postcards.

As for Della, well. She was a worker, all right, and not a cooperative one.

Sanne had been able to do little more than divert Della's attacks to her own fractured crust to deal with later, as if embedding the barbs in necrotic skin, hoping they didn't burrow deeper.

Johan had followed her and the kids inside, but quickly left for another room. A door shut. Sanne heard the dim sound of voices. He was talking to Marla.

Good.

Sanne looked around the kitchen. The kids wanted to help. She directed them with simple words and gestures.

Rufus poured a mug. Angie brought a warm, wet towel and began to clean Sanne's hands and face.

Angie's touch brought her back, just a bit. A good start.

Keyton watched intently, then opened Johan's spice drawer.

"Cinnamon?" Keyton asked.

"No," Sanne replied.

"Allspice?"

"Yes."

"Salt?"

"Definitely." Sanne smiled a bit, touched by Keyton's ingenuity.

Rufus brought a mug of hot brown liquid from a pot of coffee, holding it out. Sanne pinched a bit of dirt from her pants and sprinkled it into the coffee as she muttered a spell. Then salt and allspice.

With a strand of nettle and the twig, she stirred the concoction.

The coffee itself embodied the alchemy of land and human hand, the action it took to bring the fruit of a bush across the world, linking Sanne to all those who were part of the chain. To her kind. To humanity.

She drank.

The salt brought in the oceans of the world. The allspice would help knit her thoughts back together.

The brew tasted of dark caverns, of crashing waves. The oceans of the world flashed through her mind. She saw men and women in bright sun, picking berries, talking with each other, and singing. She felt the warmth and scent of roasting coffee beans, a mirror of humankind's accomplishment. With the allspice she felt her edges begin to repair, and was reminded of the skill of deception, ever sprinkled through the spice trade throughout history, a dash of which every magic worker must have.

She drank slowly, deliberately, feeling the liquid in her mouth and throat, then esophagus and stomach. It suffused her tissues and flowed through the rivers and rivulets of her own body. She drank down to the sludge, which she fingered out of the mug and into her mouth, completing the spell.

She handed the cup back to Rufus. The kids watched, wide-eyed.

Bit by bit, Sanne was able to slough off the turmoil and disorientation that the demon had left.

Next, she sorted out Della's attack, the swarm of barbs and shocks, discarding them with the debris of her own cracked shell.

This required motion. Sanne trembled, moving out of herself the poisonous things that were not her own, restoring to her own skin what was. She shook her entire body, arms and legs, head and tongue, making small sounds as she did.

The daze began to fall away.

When she was done, the kids stared at her with obvious concern.

"I'm all right," she assured them. "More or less," she added with a grin.

She put the mug on the sink counter, drew herself upright.

"It's time to go. Stay close. But if things go bad…"

"Don't believe everything you think," Angie said.

"Always that. Also, get flat to the ground." She did not

want them in the path of the demon. "Pretend you're a stone."

THEY WALKED TO THE ANCIENT GROVE OF TREES. Sanne was keenly aware of the gray sky in motion, of branches that drew patterns, of the cadence of birdsong.

She must be alert. The world around her would know of the approach of an otherworldly creature. A demon could not move without creating ripples, and everything would feel it, would react.

Sanne went to the ancient trees quickly, making apologies for her lack of the ritual greeting.

That was never for us, human, the center tree answered, and she could taste the whole grove's amusement.

"May I come close?"

Touch, they said.

Sanne leaned into the center tree, putting her cheek to the bark, feeling its presence, even as another part of her extended awareness to the edge of the clearing, into the ground's connecting roots and fungus, that would sense anything that smelled like demon.

"Something is coming," she told the tree softly, knowing that to tell one was to tell all. "It may want to—" there was no talking around this. "Eat you."

All things are eaten, child, the tree replied. If today is our day, we are glad of your company.

Her eyes welled with tears. She blinked them clear.

"Not today. Not if I can help it," she replied.

A tricky business, to use her power to protect the grove,

when power was exactly what the hungry young demon would want.

"At least there's only one," she muttered.

Which was plenty.

From the edge of the clearing came a crunch. A snap of twig.

Della stood, incongruous in her tan heels, beige jacket, ivory blouse with frill at the collar, against forest shadow of browns and green.

Della put a hand against the trunk of a Douglas Fir. She looked unsteady.

High heels on soft forest floor would do that to you.

Della's gaze traveled up the trunks of the great trees to the thick branches of green overhead. "These are the trees MacKenzie was willing to go into bankruptcy for? They'd make some fine cabinets."

"Ms. Meyer," Sanne said tightly. "What do you want?"

Sanne could feel Della's etheric fingers spread through the clearing. Sanne made a protective circle around the ancient trees, herself, and the kids.

The other woman smiled. "Call me Della, Susie. I insist."

Susie. No one called her that. Jerry had, once or twice, until he realized Sanne simply wouldn't answer.

Della studied Sanne. "As for what you can do for me, it's Johan we should both be concerned about. He's in trouble, and if you're truly his friend, you know that, and want what's best for him."

Della's etheric fingers were tugging at the ring Sanne had made, looking for a crack to wedge open.

No circle was perfect. She'd find it eventually. This would be a wearying game.

"You mean to give up his home and land, so you can tear it down and rip it up?" Sanne asked, as she threw a pinpoint etheric ball past and beyond Della. Just a ping, a tiny, soft sound that only an energy worker would hear.

Della looked over her shoulder, her etheric fingers pausing in their explorations.

She looked back at Sanne. "He needs this. Desperately. He's in worse shape than you know, and we're offering a once-in-a-lifetime deal. Are these trees so precious to you that you'd ruin your friend's life for them?"

The words landed and Sanne felt her emotions wobble. In that moment, Della sliced a notch out of the edge of Sanne's protective circle.

Sanne quickly knit around the cut, repairing the defense.

"I don't have time for this," Sanne said. "If I promise to call you later, will you go away now?"

"I'm not waiting, Ms. Pascrel," Della replied in an edged tone. "If your sister-lawyer convinces him to trash this deal, I'll make sure that he doesn't get another one, anywhere, goes into bankruptcy, and loses the land anyway. Is that what you want?"

Sister-lawyer. Della had researched Sanne. Of course she had.

"Of course not." Sanne swallowed building anger.

"Seems to me that a friend's future would matter to you." Della took a step toward Sanne, her heels sinking into the loam like cleats in mud. "Or is snuggling with trees more important?"

"Don't believe everything you think," Rufus whispered.

No demon here yet. Just Sanne's emotions getting the better of her.

Still, it was good advice. Sanne forced herself to refocus, sending her emotions through, letting them pass.

"Listen, Meyer," Sanne said. "A just-hatched demon is on its way here. It'll be angry, hungry, and eager to get home, using someone like you or me as a door. If it doesn't just eat us first. This isn't a safe place for you."

Della laughed. "Is that the tale you're telling these children, Pascrel?" She grinned at the three kids. "You impressed? Do you believe in Santa Claus, too?"

"We saw the thing," Angie replied.

"And you didn't," Keyton replied snottily.

Sanne frowned, took another look at Della. A power worker, yes, but one who thought demons didn't exist?

She hadn't read the books Sanne had, clearly. Maybe she didn't even know about those books.

For a moment, Sanne wondered if, when the demon came, she could maneuver it to go through Della, to make its passage home through the other woman. Sanne imagined the moment Della realized that demons did truly exist. It would be the same moment she became a corridor to another world.

But Sanne remembered what it was like to have a demon walk through her. Even that brief visit had been wretched. To willingly send the creature through the unprepared and unbelieving, like Della, would be no better than turning it on the kids.

Sanne brushed aside the flash of shame that followed the moment in which she had considered doing just that.

Suddenly Sanne saw a fly, midair, motionless and quiet. Overhead, tree branches did and did not move. Birdsong echoed.

"It's coming," Sanne yelled. "Get flat."

The kids dropped to the forest floor, craning their heads to see.

Della's smirk vanished along with her etheric questing. Her eyes widened. She looked around, confused.

The breeze died. Sound shifted, as if it were being swallowed. The gray sky darkened without changing hue.

The defensive circle Sanne had built around them would be useless against the demon. With a gesture, she dismissed it.

At the edge of the clearing was a presence. A motion. A blur.

It was here.

CHAPTER

TWENTY

Many things happened at once.

Della hobbled toward Sanne.

Angie stood from the ground. To Sanne's horror, Angie stepped between the demon and Sanne.

Rufus sprang to his feet and stood before Angie, like a goalie guarding the net.

Keyton rolled onto zir back, gaze searching overhead.

There wasn't time to yell at Angie and Rufus to get down. The creature came, fast as thought.

Sanne pulled out her mother's crystal, waving it in the air like a summoning spell.

The demon swirled. Sanne had the impression of sparkling reflections, electric current, small puffs of air. In the air was the thick, strange acrid scent of burning rubber she'd smelled on the eggs.

Through that stench, Sane momentarily glimpsed the creature's home world, where this demon was as ordinary as a rock.

Sanne couldn't even find the creature, barely finding its trail as it flashed through the air.

Della was at her side. "There." The woman pointed, then in another direction, and another.

"Not helping," Sanne snapped.

All at once a sound, sharp, like a clap of thunder. Woodsmoke came from the ancient tree by which Sanne stood. In its huge circumference was gouge, a foot deep, as if a huge, single claw had cut through softwood.

Sanne cried out. The demon was eating.

"Slow time, like you did before," Della said.

"What? Slow everything but the demon?" Sanne spared a derisive glare for Della. "Great idea."

Della scowled back, then jabbed at the air. "There."

Another crunch, another echoing crack, and another gouge in the tree, on the other side. It was not in danger of being cut in half, but if this kept up...

Della, Sanne realized, could see the demon better than she could. As Sanne followed Della's finger, dabbing the air as if throwing darts, Sanne saw ripples of motion.

Sanne deliberately stopped looking for the demon. Instead, she let the world speak to her, and tell her where the ripples were going. She saw the demon's trail, began to see where it was headed.

It was going for Rufus. He was still lurching back and forth on his toes in front of Angie, looking for something to defend against.

"I'm not afraid of you!" Angie shouted to the air, but not where the demon was. She couldn't see it.

"There," Della said to Sanne. "Let me help, damn you. Tell me what to do."

Tell me what to do.

The words landed on Sanne. She looked at Della anew, seeing an intensity, and something else she couldn't name, and hadn't seen before. Or hadn't noticed?

It was easy to think you knew a person from their fancy dry-cleaned clothes and expensive car.

But to trust her? Della had deceived MacKenzie. She had attacked Sanne.

Rufus screamed, crumpled to the ground. Keyton rolled across the ground, wrapping zir arms around him.

With a howl of rage, Angie threw something across the clearing. A rock hit a far sapling.

Yep, it was time to trust.

Sanne held out her hand to Della. An invitation.

Della didn't even hesitate. She grabbed back with a firm hold.

Sanne dropped all her protections. There was no other way. From the other woman, Sanne sensed fire, a spear-like pillar of power.

Sanne raised Della's hand in her own, weaving her fingers through Della's as she did.

"Sister," Sanne said, "make a door with me. Let's send this thing home."

Sanne felt Della's fire touch her hand, and spread through her, up and down the edge of the door their arms and bodies formed. Sanne grounded the door down into roots, soil, and the bedrock of the world.

The demon darted around the clearing, like a dog chasing chickens, or a manic child let loose in a candy shop. It bit another tree, a sapling, which snapped in half and fell.

Then the demon charged Angie. Angie stumbled backward. It flew high and wide, then turned.

Sanne felt it look at her, at the door that Sanne and Della were pumping power into, the door that was increasingly vibrant and bright.

With Sanne's free hand, she held up her mother's crystal, until she felt, like a pressure, the demon's keen attention on it.

Then she tossed the crystal through the door. The demon hatchling followed.

Sanne's ears popped with an abrupt pressure change. The ground under her seemed to shift. As the demon passed through the doorway, she felt the tug and grab of the hatchling's claws, as if it were trying to take the door with it.

They braced themselves, Sanne and Della, fingers still linked tightly together, holding steady against the tearing pull that wanted to drag them through.

Sanne lost sight and sound. She was aware of an echoing, layered silence. A place. Places, really, overlaid atop each other, drawn from energy taken from herself and Della.

Bit by bit Sanne felt the demon use her and Della to carve a pathway home.

The two of them sent power to the creature to make its path, reinforcing each other's stability as they doled out fragments of fire and earth, building blocks for the creature to make steps so that it could get home.

Then there was nothing. A fog filled Sanne's awareness. No-color, un-sound, scentlessness.

After a time, Sanne felt her own breath, and became aware of her physical body. She blinked back into the world.

Her world. Arm still raised, Della's fingers were still woven through her own.

Angie stood, just short of the door they had made, glaring through, face full of fury. She hurled a rock through the opening.

"And don't come back!" she shouted.

TWENTY-ONE

Della pulled her fingers free of Susanne's and staggered to the edge of the clearing. There, she bent over a tangle of green and brown, and threw up into the bushes.

A demon. Della had seen a demon.

When she had no more in her, she straightened, dug into her jacket pocket for her kerchief, wiped her mouth, refolded it, and turned to look back.

One of the wide-trunked trees had two bites taken out, a wedge from each side, as if a great woodsman had begun to chop it down then got distracted.

There on the forest floor, Susanne knelt, tending to a reclined child, the other two gathered close.

She was still in shock, Della realized. She had seen an actual demon.

Not only that—she had sent the damned thing home.

Helped send it home. Would have had no idea what to do without Susanne.

Della knew that the world of metaphysical practitioners was laden with fakers and frauds. Those claiming powers regularly lied, to themselves and others. Charm and bullshit was easy. Della had long ago learned to believe only what she had witnessed.

But *this* thing, she hoped never to witness again.

Her head felt fuzzy. Her stomach was not yet convinced it was empty.

And--curse it all--her hands were shaking. No, just the one that had created a door to another world.

Sister, Susanne had called her.

A small, dingy apartment. A phone call. The hospital.

Della hadn't even been allowed to see her older sister's body before they took it away. There had been no goodbyes.

None of that. Della took the familiar memory, folded it meticulously and small, and tucked it away where it belonged, with the fear and grime and toilets that never flushed right.

She breathed deep, bringing herself back to now.

With that, she turned her thoughts to Johan MacKenzie. Was the deal dead? She'd spent her own money to make it happen. Small money, but it was only small if the big money came through afterwards.

With a sigh that ended as a growl, she lurched forward toward the house. A house that should be hers now, so that she could sell it to the developers.

Her heels sunk into soft ground covered with the detritus of centuries of trees. Ruined, these shoes. Ruined.

But the deal could still happen. Della would make it happen. That was what she did: get business done.

"Della, wait," Susanne said from behind her. "A moment. Please."

TWENTY-TWO

SANNE CAUGHT UP WITH DELLA, WHO FALTERED IN her determined stride. Della gave her a mistrustful glare.

"Your kids okay?" Della asked, looking back.

"Yes. Rufus was knocked down, is all. He's fine," Susanne answered.

Della frowned. "What are they doing?"

The kids each had one hand on the tree, near the deep gashes that revealed live tissue. They were waving their other hands in the air.

Old habit made Sanne hesitate to answer this question. But why not? The other woman was no dabbler. She was a first-rate magic worker.

"Keyton had an idea, about knitting a healing for the tree," Sanne shrugged. "Worth a try. Della, I..."

Their gazes met. Della looked away, lurched forward again.

The demon must have rattled her. It made sense: Della had not believed in demons before, and now, suddenly, she must. That had to be unsettling, at best.

"Thank you," Sanne said as she followed the other woman. "You saved us. All of us."

Della paused, silent.

"If I'd had to do that alone," Sanne continued, "it would have torn me apart."

Della's puzzled look resolved into understanding. "You mean this wasn't the first time. You'd already tangled with that thing. Before you came to MacKenzie's place. That was why you were such a mess."

"Yes. And that was after we'd buried the other two demon eggs, which was no picnic."

"The other two…" Della's face went blank. "There are more?"

"Just two," Sanne said wryly. "This one was the only one that hatched. The other two are intact. And buried. Under earth, stone, and spell. Well-contained, I think. I hope."

"You hope?" Della asked incredulously.

Sanne shook her head ruefully. "Not sure what else I could have done. None of the books even hinted that two workers together could make a demon-door that kept them both safe. I don't think any of the sages knew that."

"I have business," Della said flatly, stumbling forward again.

Della's reactions were puzzling to Sanne. What was Sanne missing? She looked at Della again, trying for a deeper read.

There it was: an old wound, like a dim red scar, shimmered beneath the surface of Della's spirit.

A child's wound. The loss of love ripped away.

Sanne stayed close as Della struggled to walk through forest in her heels.

"You've given me knowledge that maybe no one else has," Sanne said. "That a demon-door can be made that doesn't destroy the maker. I owe you my life."

Della gave her a cold smile. "Suits me. Come along, tell MacKenzie to let the deal go through."

"I can't let you take the trees," Sanne said. "I owe you, but not that."

"Then get your damned scarf off him, and let me finish my business."

"I can't just—"

"No? Then your debt is worthless." Della strode toward the house, stomping her heels into the ground.

"You thought demons didn't exist," Sanne said urgently. "Now you do. Give me a moment to show you something else you might not know about."

Della came to an abrupt stop, lips tight.

A deep wound. Something that had shaped her from very young.

Fire flashed in Sanne's memory. She understood.

"What do you want, Meyer?" Sanne asked quietly, putting into the question a gentle but obvious spell of possibility, like a dusting of light. "What do you really want?"

"An Azimut 72 yacht. In silver," Della said.

Sanne suppressed a smirk, but Della caught it, and lashed back with power.

As an attack, it lacked intent to harm. More like an angry flick. Sanne parried, let it go by.

Suddenly, Sanne was tired of conflict. "I mean the thing that you want, that money can't buy. What is it?"

"What do you care, Susanne?"

Sanne reflected on this day, the courage of the kids, the strangeness of a demon hatchling, and the power of unity to send it home.

With Della.

"Sanne," Sanne said gently to the other woman. "That's what my friends and family call me. Would you, too?"

Della swallowed, her face showing emotion held tightly in check. She turned to look, not at Sanne, but back at the trees.

After a long moment, she spoke.

"All right. Sanne. Show me this something else."

TWENTY-THREE

Sanne walked back to the trees, slowly, wordlessly, hoping Della would follow. She did. As they approached, the kids backed away to give them the space.

Smart kids, Sanne thought fondly.

Sanne put a hand on the deeply furrowed bark of the center tree, seeing how the energy swirled around the gouges in its side, the wounds beginning to knit. The kids had done well.

Della stopped behind her, short of the surrounding gnarled roots that made an apron at the base of the tree.

"I grieve for your wounds," Sanne mouthed to the tree.

We are eaten. Yet we remain. We will heal.

Sanne looked at Della. "Did you hear that?"

Della shook her head.

If Della could not hear the trees, then she would never understand. Sanne studied her for a moment, judged her willing to try.

"This person," Sanne said to her trees, "is my friend." It

was hard to make the words true, but she must. "My friend," she repeated, imbuing the words with intention, like a spell cast within, on herself.

It was not enough. Sanne shut her eyes and went within to find the places of anger and resentment, where Della's actions and words had landed. She touched those spots. Some were sore. She let them melt and flow, past her feet, down and down, where they might be absorbed into the embrace of the living earth.

Under her fingers, Sanne felt the ancient tree's skin.

"Will you speak to my friend?" Sanne whispered.

In the quiet moment that followed, Sanne opened her eyes. She heard the buzz of a fly, a hawk's distant cry, the creaking of branches overhead in the wind.

"Well, I'll be damned," Della whispered.

Joy flooded Sanne. She smiled.

Sanne herself hadn't heard it; whatever the trees had said to Della had been private.

Della's expression changed to one that Sanne had not seen before. An openness. Something bordering on wonder.

Now Della pulled off her heeled shoes, tossing them aside. In bare stockings, she stepped forward tentatively, picking her way across the gnarled roots to the base of the tree. There she leaned her forehead against it and closed her eyes.

Sending a demon back home? Easy, compared to getting someone to hear something they didn't think could speak.

Or for one person to see another more fully?

She watched as Della leaned against the tree. Della's red scar intensified, became bright, spread, faded, and at last vanished.

BACK AT THE HOUSE, SANNE COULD SEE THAT Johan's conversation with Marla had left him ready to revoke the contract.

Della pulled Sanne aside. They stood across the yard from the others, by an apple tree full of blossoms.

"You have your magic," Della said quietly. "I have mine. Tell MacKenzie to let the contract stand. Give me three days to come back with a new contract that supersedes it. One that will protect the trees no matter who owns the land."

"Let the contract stand as is?"

Della nodded. "I need time to set up a new one, while I keep the developers' confidence."

Sanne searched the other woman's face. "It's not that I don't trust you…"

"You don't. I get it." Della pulled her even closer, voice dropping. "How's this: state law allows Johan unilateral right to terminate within five days. Your sister-lawyer will have the appropriate form. Get him to sign and notarize it, but keep it to himself. If I don't deliver, he can end the contract."

Sanne considered. Della was not wrong that Johan needed a deal that let him take care of himself and his parents.

From across the yard, Johan watched the two women, as if waiting to see who would win.

Della gave Sanne a wolfish smile. "This is my forte, Pascrel. Give me three days."

"All right, Meyer."

They shook hands.

Della and Terry left Sanne to explain to Johan and Marla what the two women had in mind.

Then Sanne drove the kids back to their respective homes. To each, she would give a twig or stem to take with them.

"Study those," she said as she drove. "Show and tell your parents what a great time you had wildcrafting this afternoon."

"Oh, I see," said Rufus. "Smooth."

It had been anything but smooth. But she knew what Rufus meant.

"Who knew plants could be so exciting?" asked Ketyon from the back seat.

"I learned way more than I expected to," Angie said, quite sincerely. "Some things I hope I never learn again."

"The other two eggs," Keyton asked. "They're not going to hatch out, Sanne, are they?"

Sanne pulled into the driveway of Angie's home, turned off the engine.

"As long as they're not disturbed," Sanne answered.

There was an uneasy silence.

"Thing is," Keyton said, "if one of those ever got loose in Marigold..."

"I'm proud of you--that was the best crocheting I've

ever seen," Sanne replied with a grin. Then, more soberly. "I think the earth will hold them. I do."

"It had better," Angie said. "Or I'm going to need some bigger rocks."

CHAPTER

TWENTY-FOUR

Della called the meeting. She arrived last, pulling her car in behind Terry's blue Mustang, noting with some amusement that he had somehow found time to wash and wax his ride. MacKenzie's dirty, beat-up white pickup truck was next to the house. Alongside that was Sanne's ancient little Nissan.

Della had heard the Nissan's engine last time she was here, as Sanne drove away. The car was on its last legs. It must run on magic.

The four of them stood at MacKenzie's kitchen table. Someone had been cooking this morning, and the room smelled like eggs and bacon and coffee. Della declined MacKenzie's offer of a cup of his drip, not wanting to replace the memory of her own near-perfect latte from earlier.

She rolled out maps on the table, using her long pink fingernail to indicate the area around the forested part of the land on a plat map.

"The trees and the surrounding forest," she told them.

"Held in common by tenants in perpetuity. Unde-velopable."

Sanne frowned. "That's what your last contract said, no?"

Della looked at MacKenzie, who seemed cautiously hopeful, and Terry, whose expression told her that he still didn't understand what Della was doing.

"A little change to the specific wording," Della replied.

An understatement if there ever was one; over the last three days, Della had rewritten the entire contract from scratch. The vague parts were now as solid as stone.

"What about the developers?" Sanne asked.

Della gave the other witch a smile. "Met with them yesterday. I've laid out a plan for them to make their high-end houses attractive to rich millennials with environmental leanings. They're on-board. They get it now."

Della had done a bit more than that. She would clear far less from this deal than she had intended.

And that was the strangest part. In the mirror this morning, putting on her earrings, touching up her eyes, she had stopped to stare. Who was this woman, going to bat for a bunch of old trees?

Trees that spoke. Trees that healed. Sanne's words came back to her: *The thing that you want, that money can't buy.* Frankly, Della felt good. She had not felt this good in a long time.

"It's a better contract, then?" MacKenzie asked. His tone was wrapped in doubt, tinged with hope.

Della handed him a folder of papers. "I'll send an electronic version, too. Have Sanne's sister-lawyer look it over. Or whoever you like."

Johan took the papers bemusedly.

Della gave a wry smile. There was rich irony in this moment; MacKenzie was no longer wearing Sanne's scarf. The damned thing hung from an old hook at the door.

That meant that if Della had not invited Sanne this morning—if Della had not changed the MacKenzie contract and the developer contracts, at great expense—this would be the moment to congratulate MacKenzie on the former contract. She could have walked away with everything she wanted.

Had wanted.

Oh well. Yachts were too much trouble anyway.

"Offer's good for five business days, Mr. MacKenzie," Della said in a businesslike tone. "I'd like to direct your attention to a few new clauses that give you both right of first refusal on two of the new construction houses."

Della waited for Sanne to register the words. The other woman looked up from studying the map.

"What?" she asked.

"You could live here, Pascrel," Della said.

Sanne snorted. "Won't they sell for something like a million?"

"Oh, more than that," Della said dryly.

Sanne shook her head. "I'm dirt poor, Meyer."

"I could help, Susanne," MacKenzie said earnestly. "I mean, after this all finishes up, I'll have some money. Right?"

"You'll need it, Johan." Sanne's eyes flickering momentarily to Della. "And when it's done, it might not be as much as you think."

"Oh," MacKenzie said.

Della had a very good idea of just how much it would be. MacKenzie would be fine.

There was nothing more to do now but let MacKenzie and his lawyer, whoever it was, look it over. Della knew that he would sign this time, and it would stick; it was everything he wanted and more.

They shook hands all around, a strange formality, given what they'd been through together.

Della left the house, Terry following. The spring morning was chilly, but warming quickly, the sun bright across the trees and farms that stretched up into the hills, where more old farms were not being used.

More opportunities. In her mind, new strategies were playing out.

"Babe?" Terry asked softly. "Is this really a good deal? Because it doesn't seem like one to me."

"It is," Della said, giving his shoulder an affectionate squeeze.

She had watched as Terry went over the numbers last night, increasingly dubious, but she'd convinced him this was part of the longer game here in Marigold, to establish herself as the only broker who could successfully pry this sort of property from entrenched old farmers, and hand it off to developers to build new homes for new money.

Not entirely a lie.

Terry went to his Mustang, leaned against the rich blue door, checking his phone.

MacKenzie and Sanne came out of the house. MacKenzie had the scarf again wrapped around his neck. He smiled and waved, seeming happy.

Terry looked up, waved back at MacKenzie. "You ever

want to take my ride out again, Johan, you just—" he raised his phone. "Call me."

Della stood by her own car, which gleamed bright magenta in the morning sun. She scrolled through her messages.

"Here, take this," she heard MacKenzie say.

"Oh, nice," Terry replied.

Della wasn't paying attention. Then she was.

By the time she looked up to see what they were talking about, MacKenzie was already at the Mustang, wrapping the scarf around Terry's neck.

Della closed the distance as fast as she could, but it was too late.

Terry gripped the scarf's tails tightly, let out a howl, and bent double. A shocked MacKenzie backed away.

The years of protections Della had woven around Terry shredded and came apart like wet tissue paper. Not because they weren't strong—they were as formidable as Della could make them—but the spells relied on Terry's own powerful will to keep them solid and tight.

In a moment, the cursed scarf had cut through it all.

Terry's expression went bleak, horrified. He began to moan.

Della pulled the scarf from him, hurled it to the ground. As it fell, it dragged from Terry the rest of his insulating spells, dissipating them into the earth.

Terry sat heavily on the damp grass. He looked up at her, with the vulnerable and fearful face of an injured child.

"I'm here, baby," she said, dropping next to him. She wrapped him in her arms. He buried his face in her shoulder.

Sanne crouched down some paces away.

"What happened?" Sanne mouthed to Della.

"You and your damned scarf," Della hissed back.

Terry was sobbing into her shoulder. His words were muffled. "My fault. All my fault."

"No, it wasn't. You didn't know."

He pulled his head back and stared, his look haunted. "Didn't I? I dared her. Called her a coward. Then I left. Forgot she was there. The car backed up. Over her, Della. 'Coward,' was the last thing anyone said to her. That was me. I'm a monster."

"Baby, it was an accident," Della said.

"Was it?" Terry looked away from Della to MacKenzie. "Was it?"

MacKenzie looked shocked to have this question put to him. He walked over to the scarf, picked it up thoughtfully. "I don't know, Terry. When I feel like that, I pray." He shrugged. "Maybe you do something else. I think sometimes things aren't so simple. We can't work 'em out on our own. We need help." He brushed the grass and dirt from the scarf and held it out to Terry. "You ever want someone to talk to, I'm here."

Terry seemed to digest this. At last, he nodded, and got to his feet, taking the scarf from MacKenzie.

Della stood, twitching and considering all sorts of spells, as Terry put the damned, long thing around his neck again. But something made her hesitate.

Let him, she decided. Maybe it was time.

Terry gave a shuddering exhale, and looked around, his gaze landing on Della.

"I got a question," he said to her.

"Sure, babe. What is it?"

"No diamond big enough," he muttered.

"What?" she asked.

"Why would you marry someone like me?" he asked. "Why?"

The question, voiced at last.

Della brushed cut grass and dirt from her now quite-stained pastel pink trousers. When was she going to learn not to come out here with good clothes?

She struggled to sort out how she felt about this question and Terry's intense tone. With an audience, no less. A business audience.

Mostly business. Business and something else, which was also confusing.

Normally, she would shut this conversation down. Make it into a joke. *Good one, Terry. Let's talk later.*

But that wasn't quite who she was now.

She took a moment to consider, then she gestured around the space.

"This, Terry. You care about a girl you hardly knew. You're a kinder person than I'll ever be. You wonder, are you at fault for what happened." Della shook her head. "Not an easy question, as Mr. MacKenzie rightly says. But you're brave enough to ask it." She took a breath, asked herself the other question he hadn't quite asked. "It would be nice if you could chew gum with your mouth closed, but even so, yes, I'd marry you. And that's why: you're kind and you're brave."

Terry's look shifted to astonishment. He dug into a pocket with scrabbling fingers and brought out a small box.

"This is for you," he said. "I hope."

The small velvet box was covered in pocket lint and something that might have once been a bit of chewed gum. How long had Terry been carrying that around, trying to work up the nerve for this moment?

Della felt oddly touched. She opened the box.

This wasn't quite how the ritual was supposed to go, she knew, and that made her oddly happy. She took out the ring, admiring the diamond as it caught sunlight and returned it to her eyes in brilliant colors. She gestured Terry close, took his hand, and slipped the ring on his smallest finger.

"But—" he began.

"Will you marry me, Terrance Hundley? Be my mate, in legality and formality, with suitable pomp and extravagance, as soon as we can arrange to rent the Marigold town hall?"

"Oh," he breathed. "Yes. I will."

"Good. Shall I wear this lovely thing for a while?"

"Oh. Yes, please."

She smiled. He took off the ring, and eagerly put it on her ring finger. It fit perfectly.

MacKenzie began to clap. Sanne joined him.

Della threaded her arm through Terry's. "If you don't mind, I'd like to take my fiancé for a walk. There's a special place I want to show him."

"You bet," MacKenzie said.

TWENTY-FIVE

Once again home, Sanne was covered in the dirt of a long day's work at the land, which she had done after Della and Terry left.

One look at Terry's face when he and Della had come back from their time with the trees and Sanne knew something wonderful had happened for him. He looked like a changed man, his expression open and full of tenderness. Then the two of them had gone back to town to celebrate their engagement.

Sanne had decided to celebrate in her own way, digging in the dirt, and talking with plants and trees.

At home, Sanne looked at her dirt-covered palms. There, in the pattern of earth and skin, she saw two lines and three dots. A symbol of spring, of renewal. Of life.

She looked around the space in which she lived. Her one-room house had become quite cluttered these last weeks. Borrowed library books in need of returning. Spools of wire. Various tools. The metal tackle box. Needles for knitting and crocheting. Unwashed dishes. A half-eaten bar of chocolate.

She snapped off a piece. As it the melted in her mouth, she continued her visual inventory.

The shelves were similarly cluttered. And the floor... stray packing peanuts had found their way under the bed. Somehow, you never got them all.

At least there was one less thing to put away: her mother's crystal, thrown through the door to another world, to draw the demon home. Sanne felt certain that her mother would have approved.

In any case, it was time to get to it and clean up. Where to start?

To clean one's own space, always a reflection of one's internal world, was itself a form of magic. To address it simplistically or meticulously was a mistake—one would end up with a space that was visually clear, but still energetically cluttered.

One must study the world as it was, if one wanted to understand it. Especially one's own world.

Sanne let her focus go soft. She looked for energy flows, for places of motion and stagnation. She walked the room, gazing across herbs hanging overhead, various rocks and crystals, bottles of sand and powder.

She trailed her fingers over the spines of many books, notebooks, and recipe books that held deeper lore.

There.

She felt it before she knew what it was, the hard knot of stagnant energy in the room.

An envelope. The letter that Jerry had sent her.

Ah, crap.

She wrestled internally. Yes, this was a place that needed cleaning, but her deep anger of betrayal was like a huge boulder in the way.

Jerry had burned her books. He had mocked her, and had dismissed what she knew to be true. He had made her feel like an outcast in her own home.

There was nothing he could say now to make that right. Only more wrong.

Still, she had to read it, to let the bastard speak from the grave. Even if his words were shallow, cutting, and cruel.

Afterwards, though, she would burn the letter until it was fine ash. A fitting end. A suitable cleansing.

Or...she could burn it first.

"No, no, none of that," she muttered to herself, taking the cursed thing in hand.

Sanne cast a spell on herself as she sat in a chair, one of calm, quiet, and openness. She trickled her energy into the ground, into the bedrock, so that the earth could help her by taking whatever Jerry could send.

With a deep breath, she opened the envelope and began to read.

Dear Susanne,

Your mother was good with words. I'm not. You were, too. You were so like her.

Your mother was also my sister. I missed her more than I ever let on. I was a wreck when I got you two. I had to take care of you, so I tried to pretend I was fine. But I was a terrible parent. I let myself get angry at you children, instead of dealing with my own grief.

That was wrong. I'm sorry.

I'm sorry about your books. That was wrong, too.

I asked Marla to send you all your mother's things. I should have done it long ago.

Here are a couple more things. One I can't read. Maybe you can. The other I've been tending to for you for a long time. Now it's yours.

Try to forgive me. Not for me, but for you.

Another thing I never said: I'm proud of you for fighting back. You were brave.

Your mother would be proud, too.

Jerry.

By his signature on the paper was a spot, slightly dimpled, as if it had been wet.

Sanne touched it, got a whiff of Jerry and a sense of deep sorrow. A tear. He had shed a tear while writing this letter.

A mirroring sadness welled in Sanne. She sniffled, blinking her eyes clear, and opened the next envelope. It contained a folded note in her mother's handwriting, in the private code they shared.

As she read, Sanne realized that this was the note that had once accompanied the demon eggs. It told how very dangerous they were, and how important it was to keep them in the enchanted metal box in which they were stored. Had been stored, until Marla opened that metal box and sent the contents—the twine-wrapped cardboard box that contained demon eggs—to Sanne.

The three eggs, her mother wrote, had been in Sanne's family for generations. Both a curse and a trust, to be held secure, away from the world, at all costs.

The mystery of how the family had gotten the eggs and

became their custodian was in another book in the family's library.

Probably one that Jerry had burned.

But wait. *Storage units*, her sister had said. Could the book be in one of them? Maybe it wasn't gone.

That got Sanne thinking. What else might be in storage, tucked into an old box, wrapped in enchanted fabric, or sealed into a jar? Sanne would need to call her sister to talk, and soon.

She held the letter that her mother had penned and felt a familiar grief. Her mother had not known what to do with the eggs, beyond to keep them contained. Sanne had needed to figure out what to do with one that hatched.

Your mother would be proud.

Jerry might be right about that.

At last, Sanne opened the final envelope that Jerry had sent. It contained a few folded and printed papers, newer than her mother's note.

Atop them, a sticky note in Jerry's handwriting read:

Your parents set this up for you when they were alive. It's been compounding returns for over two decades. I added some more. Use it well.

It was a brokerage statement in Sanne's name.

Sanne gaped. There was money in the account. A lot of money.

CHAPTER

TWENTY-SIX

DELLA COULD SENSE THE FLOW OF MONEY. SHE could sense the way it swirled around and through the world, moving through legal contracts in rivulets or streams or sometimes rivers.

She had predicted that the MacKenzie deal would go through. She had felt it. She had been right.

MacKenzie had signed. The five-day review period passed uneventfully.

Developer A had signed, too.

Everyone was happy. Even Terry, who was busy planning the wedding.

"I don't know if I can get it all done," he said, words that should have been a complaint, but weren't. He smiled broadly as he spoke, then gave her his delicious smoldering look.

Terry had changed. His distracted manner had turned bright and clear, his smile infectious.

Did Della, he wanted to know, want to invite Susanne

179

Pascrel? How about Johan MacKenzie, who Terry now considered a friend?

Yes, Della had replied. Yes to both. Yes to all. What the heck—invite Sanne's students and parents, too. Invite everyone. It would be a party.

Della laughed a little at herself. Terry wasn't the only one who was changed.

She opened her laptop, thick stacks of signed contracts at her side, and scanned through various online records, keeping track, checking in.

Construction prices. Social media chatter. Developer group discussion. Typically, when Della made a land sale, she moved on, having her cash in hand and needing no more to do with the matter.

This was different. She had given up big money for control. Among other things, Della had reserved final approval on the location of roads and sidewalks, something she could only do with a developer who trusted her to be sensible about it.

An odd thing to get involved with, so she had needed to spin it hard, with durable spells that convinced Developer A that it was in their interest to give it to her.

The real reason, of course, was that there were two spots on the property that Della needed to be sure were deeply buried, covered with more than enough dirt and gravel, and sealed with cement and powerful magic. Those spots would turn into roadway, perhaps. Or sidewalks. Not houses.

Whatever they became, Della would see to it that the stones that Sanne had put atop the two demon eggs would not ever be turned over.

Della also checked the assisted living facility receipts, to be sure that MacKenzie's parents were seen to. It was increasingly clear that MacKenzie was not interested in buying a house in the new development on his old property. He wanted to live in town, closer to his parents.

So Della had found him a listing of suitable apartments nearby.

As for the scarf... she made a thoughtful noise and glanced at where it now lived, on the coat rack by the penthouse door. Some days Terry wore it, even when it was too warm. Sometimes he'd talk to himself softly, as if he were sorting things out. But even when he took it off, he seemed more himself than ever.

Della considered the long, garish red, orange, and green thing, and wondered what it would be like to try it on.

Maybe some other day.

Her cell rang. The ring sound carried the distinct tone of money. So while Della was surprised to hear Sanne's voice on the other end, asking for advice, she was unsurprised to hear that the topic was an unexpected inheritance.

Della grinned as she explained the fundamentals of money management to Sanne who had probably never had as much as a month's rent extra in her pocket, and the advantages of investing in real estate. Especially if you were living in the place.

Why yes, Della replied, Sanne could have a great deal of input on a house before plans were complete. Yes, Della would be happy to help with that.

As Della spoke, she paged through the MacKenzie contract, admiring her handiwork. If MacKenzie didn't want a house on his old land, that was fine with Della; she had tucked another clause into the very long contract, one that also allowed Della right of first refusal.

It might be good to have Sanne as a neighbor. Convenient, too, if the other two eggs ever got it into their minds to consider hatching.

Also, Sanne knew a thing or two that Della was interested in learning about.

A small town, this, but there was a lot here for Della beyond money.

Might be good to start making longer term plans. Della had a feeling she and Terry would be in Marigold for a while.

TWENTY-SEVEN

THE KIDS WERE TAPPING AWAY EAGERLY ON THEIR laptops as Sanne drank a cup of cold-yet-truly-marvelous coffee.

Since getting her inheritance, Sanne had discovered that really good coffee tasted good even at room temperature. And now she could afford it.

Ironically, she'd figured out how to brew it without a coffee maker. No more cleaning plastic. No more discardable filters. Just a good old-fashioned tempered glass jar, a thin wood stick, hot water, and time.

That was the best part that the inheritance bought her: time. She could do the work she wanted, and skip the other gigs that helped her scrape by.

Coffee had never tasted so good.

"There," said Rufus, sitting back smugly, as if he'd won a race.

Sanne set her cup on the counter, and strolled to the table. "Yeah? Show me."

Rufus turned his laptop to reveal a picture the kids had

taken when they were recently out on the land. It was fire-weed, thick with magenta flowers. Under it was a description Rufus had written of its various uses. It needed a bit of editing, but it was basically correct.

Unsurprisingly, since it was Rufus, he mostly wrote about how to eat it.

Angie and Keyton, on either side, craned their heads to see.

"Mine's Devil's Club," said Keyton. "You can eat that, too."

"Really?" Angie asked Sanne.

"Well," Sanne said, "technically yes, but it's a bit of work and a touch dangerous until you know what you're doing. Also, native tribes had different names for this sacred plant. Might be good to include those, too."

"Oh! Research! I'm on it," Keyton said, eagerly tapping on zir keyboard.

Sanne had made the suggestion and the three teenagers had jumped on it: build a website with links to social media where other kids their age could post pictures of plants, help each other identify them, and talk about how to use them. Or eat them.

Sanne had pointed out that once they had a few dozen plants up, with clear pictures and descriptions, they could work a point system into the code and turn it into a game.

"Oh!" Keyton said. "Show us how to put in Easter eggs."

"Easter eggs?" Angie frowned.

"The ones little kids hunt for? Like next weekend, at my church?" asked Rufus.

"Not that," Keyton said.

"Then what?" Rufus asked.

"Something in the game. Something to find," Keyton answered.

"That's already the point of the game, to find the right plant," Rufus said, looking slightly annoyed.

Keyton shook zir head. "An Easter egg is an extra. Like if you chord three keys and you get a love potion or something."

Now Sanne had the attention of all three kids.

"A love potion?" Rufus asked. "Is that a real thing?"

"Pretty real," Sanne said, nodding.

"Does it work?" asked Angie.

"Usually," Sanne replied, managing to keep a straight face.

"Tell us how," said Keyton.

Sanne pulled up a chair, and sat, her hands creating shapes in the air as she described the potion. "Leaf of Hawthorn, petal of Wild Rose, and a lavender flower."

"Go on," said Keyton.

"Next," Sanne said, "find the person you want to cast the spell on. Bring them their favorite beverage. With me so far?"

They all nodded eagerly.

"Sit down with the person who is the object of your spell. Ask them questions. Listen to what they say. Tell them something genuine about yourself. The spell has begun."

Angie was suppressing a smile.

"Wait," Keyton said, "you mean you have to talk to them?"

"No, no," Rufus said. "What about plants? The potion? The magic?"

"You are the magic, Rufus. Being there, being truly present with someone, that's the magic."

"Oh, like we are," Angie said, her expression turning thoughtful. "The four of us."

That caught Sanne by surprise. But Angie wasn't wrong.

"Yeah," said Keyton. "We did magic together. Here. In the forest. Real magic."

The kids looked at each other shyly, grins coming to their faces.

Angie bounded out of her chair, went to the counter, and brought back Sanne's cup, holding it out to her.

Sanne felt herself blush slightly. She accepted the cup.

"Okay, back to the Easter Eggs," Keyton said.

Angie sat and started typing on her computer. "Hawthorn. Wild Rose."

"They won't hatch out something weird, these Easter eggs, will they?" Rufus asked.

"Not if we're the ones coding them," Angie replied confidently.

"Probably not," Sanne agreed.

Sanne raised her cup of cold brew in a toast to the three teenagers. She took a sip, watching them over the lip of the mug as they looked back.

"Let's find out," she said.

A MESSAGE FROM THE AUTHOR

Thanks for joining me on this adventure!

When you read a story, you are an essential part of what makes it come alive. If you liked this story, say so. Tell others. Tell me, even! We authors do our best work when we know it's touched someone.

Ratings also make a huge difference. A note to a friend, a good review, a rating—these are precious gifts that also help us create more stories. Thank you!

ALSO BY SONIA ORIN LYRIS

"Treasure Twice Over," *Witches, Cutter's Final Cut: Issue Four.* Join Sanne for some magical adventure in the Marigold library!

The Seer Saga, (The Seer, Unmoored, Maelstrom, Landfall), an immersive high fantasy series

Better Selves, a collection of science fiction and urban fantasy stories, with afterword by Barry N. Malzberg

"When Strangers Meet," Dispatches from Anarres, tales in tribute to Ursula K. Le Guin

ABOUT THE AUTHOR

Sonia Orin Lyris writes stories about strong women and the men who can see them. Her writing has been called "immersive" and "unsparing."

She is the author of *The Seer Saga*, an epic high-fantasy series that asks questions about power and love. She is co-creator of *Rochi*, a divination and gambling game with vivid artwork.

Her hobbies include partner dance, martial arts, fine chocolate, and feline poetry.

WANT MORE?

Follow me on Patreon for juicy notes, or subscribe for confessional posts. https://www.patreon.com/lyris

For concise updates, check my Facebook feed. https://www.facebook.com/authorlyris

My newsletter is infrequent but excellently informative. Sign up here. https://lyris.org/subscribe/

All my newest works, all in one place: https://lyris.org/newly-published/

More at my website. https://lyris.org/